TRASH is part of a threesome of Southeast Asian urban anthologies. The other two are called **FLESH** and **HEAT**. We chose to interpret 'urban' as a state of mind rather than population count or infrastructural development, so a few of these stories and essays take place in very remote places indeed. But they shake it up, they twist and shout, they wanna show you what it's all about.

About FIXI NOVO

Fixi Novo is the English-language (but American-spelling) imprint of Buku Fixi, a Malaysian publishing company.

In 2014, Buku Fixi won an award for Adult Trade Publishing at the London Book Fair. Despite the name of the award, it is not directly related to the porn industry.

In 2016, Fixi Novo decided to also start publishing short stories and novels from the rest of Southeast Asia. Perhaps we could be the publishing equivalent of AirAsia, or even of pink plastic bags.

We primarily look for urban contemporary pulp fiction. To be informed of any future anthology calls, do follow us at fb.com/fixinovo.

Only those accepted into any of our anthologies will be invited to submit full-length works.

TRASH

A SOUTHEAST ASIAN URBAN ANTHOLOGY

EDITED BY
DEAN FRANCIS ALFAR
& MARC DE FAOITE

Published by
Fixi Novo *which is an imprint of:*
Buku Fixi (002016254-V)
B-8-2A Opal Damansara, Jalan PJU 3/27
47810 Petaling Jaya, Malaysia
info@fixi.com.my
http://fixi.com.my

TRASH: A Southeast Asian Urban Anthology

Editors: Dean Francis Alfar & Marc de Faoite

First Printing: April 2016

Cover artwork by: instagram.com/moribayu
(Based on an idea by Angeline Woon)
Layout: Teck Hee
Consultants: Lee Ee Leen & Amir Muhammad

ISBN 978-967-0954-38-7
Catalogue-in-Publication Data available from the National Library of Malaysia.

Printed by:
Vinlin Press Sdn Bhd
2 Jalan Meranti Permai 1, Meranti Permai Industrial Park
Batu 15, Jalan Puchong, 47100 Puchong, Malaysia

ALSO AVAILABLE:

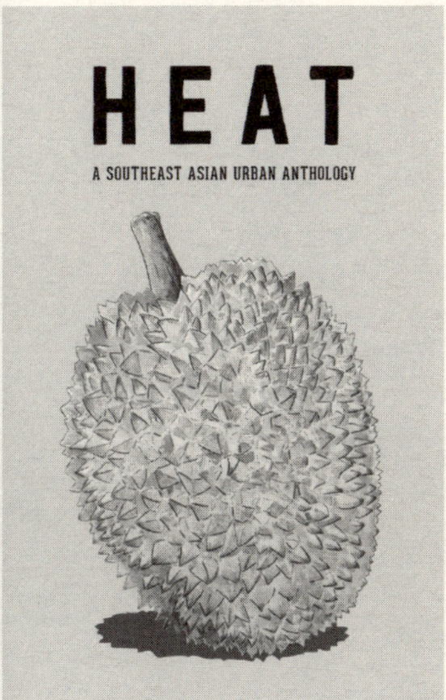

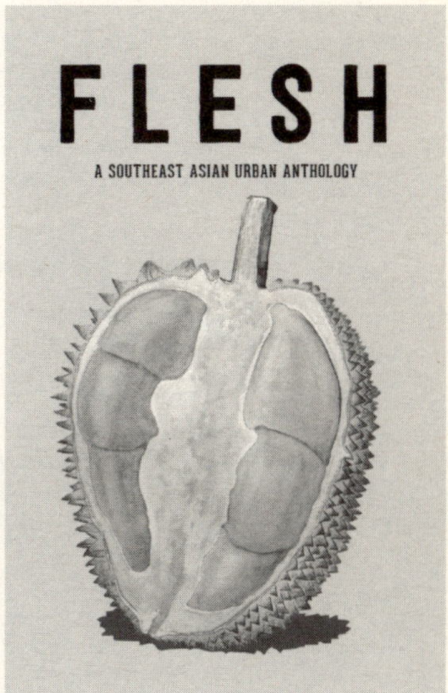

PUBLICATION CREDITS

"Mrs. Chandra's War Against Dust" was first published in *New Village 4* (Malaysia, September 2013).

"The Hunger Houses" first appeared in the Multiethnic issue of the web magazine Innsmouth Free Press on 1 June 2010.

"Baby's Breath" was first published in *A Rainbow Feast: New Asian Short Stories* (Marshall Cavendish, Kuala Lumpur, 2010).

"How to Make White People Happy" was first published in *The Los Angeles Review*, Issue 8 (USA, 2010) and nominated for the Pushcart Nonfiction Prize.

"Flowers for KK" was first published in *KL Noir : White* edited by Amir Hafizi (Fixi Novo, Malaysia, 2013).

CONTENTS

INTRO

DEAN FRANCIS ALFAR:

Writers from all over South East Asia responded to the call for submissions for this anthology with stories inspired by or about trash. Co-editor Marc de Faoite and I had the happy task of reading each story and seeing for ourselves how authors from diverse cultures and backgrounds interpreted the challenge.

For a few, trash was just trash: refuse and rubbish were prominent in their stories, the discarded remnants of the used and unwanted spun into the lives of their characters.

For others, trash was a representation of excess, a signifier for environmental despoilment, the very picture of poverty. Trash littered streets filled with violence brought about by imbalance of wealth and nature.

Some told stories of wasted lives and used-up opportunities, of tainted relationships or obsolete modes of thinking best thrown away, and of social or cultural pollution.

Some spun trash in a positive way, recognizing the worth in the worthless, and seeing second chances in the castoffs of other people.

We read and selected those that impressed us the most, those stories that elevated discourse or resonated the most or made us think or simply blew us away.

In each of the stories between these covers, there is a definite sense of place and a powerful point of view.

Local color abounds in the setting of many of these stories, situating and contextualizing the narrratives and thus becoming an integral part of what makes them work so well.

English is the main language platform but the names, idioms and turns of phrase are reflective of cultures where it is not the primary language – where it fails, local languages step forward with confidence.

With contributors from Malaysia, Singapore, the Philippines, Indonesia, and India, we are happy to present an anthology that showcases varied perspectives and insights on the nature of trash.

Read and enjoy.

— Manila, *March 2016*

MARC DE FAOITE:

As a child, the weekly visit from the growling garbage truck held a particular fascination for me, but the bin men were an unruly lot and never put the lids back on the rubbish bins - apparently a source of some irritation to my mother. While other boys my age wanted to be astronauts or firemen I aspired to a career in trash collection, and confided in my mother that I would assiduously replace the lid of every rubbish bin I emptied.

That particular career plan never panned out. Yet forty years later I found myself submerged in 'trash' – in this case some hundred and twenty stories from throughout South East Asia and beyond, submitted for this collection. As the reader will soon discover, there were gems to be found among this 'trash', most of which shone on their own, and a few that needed just a little polishing.

Together with co-editor Dean Francis Alfar we tried as much as possible to respect the integrity of the stories, allowing the writers their own voices, rather than forcing them into homogenized enunciations that would please devotees of Messrs. Strunk & White. The voices in this collection are colorful, with some of the writers bravely working through the filter of a second language. Even those that aren't are still influenced (to a greater or lesser degree) by the inflections and accents of the different languages spoken in their respective lands - for example in Zedeck Siew's "Mrs. Chandra's War Against Dust", there is a deliberate effort to replicate the colloquial English used by sections of Malaysia's ethnic Indians. To add further authentic local spice and flavor, as per Fixi Novo's mission statement, colloquialisms and phrases in South East Asian languages have neither been italicized or translated.

The stories included vary in style and theme, but one that I will single out here for attention is Victor Fernando R. Ocampo's "Pantopticon", and in particular his use of Spivak pronouns. The reader may already be familiar with Spivak pronouns, but even though they have been around since the mid-1970s (about the same time I was planning a career in garbage collection) I had never encountered them before, and at first mistakenly attributed the "e, eir, em" formulations in Victor's story to a faulty keyboard.

"I wanted to force the reader to come to terms with the micro-aggressions of their own gender marking preferences," said Victor during one of our conversations on the subject.

This sensitivity to gender issues - and subjects more political and personal, pursued by other writers in this collection - captures the zeitgeist of the rapidly changing societies and communities of South East Asia. These writers have sorted through the 'trash' and found things that can be valued as still useful, things that deserve to be salvaged, and recycled, or reused, but they also point unflinchingly at structures, strictures, and modes of thought that have clearly served their time and must be discarded and thrown out on the rubbish heap. Enjoy.

— Langkawi, *March 2016*

MRS. CHANDRA'S WAR AGAINST DUST

ZEDECK SIEW

Down on her knees, Mrs. Chandra squeezes her left eye shut and presses her cheek to the floor.

The marble is covered in tiny particles. She wipes it with a finger, and her finger comes away smudged with a line of gray and black.

"Dusty, so dusty!" Mrs. Chandra says. "And I just swept and mopped yesterday!"

It is always extra dusty, nowadays. Because of the construction work: down the hill, on the main road there. They tore down all the shophouses – where Tan Brothers and her favorite sundry shop used to be – and now they are building a supermarket.

The front door opens. Mrs. Chandra looks up and sees Mr. Chandra wander in, absorbed in his morning paper. His sandals are still strapped to his feet.

She chases him out the door with a broom.

Down on her knees, Mrs. Chandra presses her cheek to the floor and squeezes her right eye shut.

The marble is covered in dust. She wipes it with a hand, and her palm comes away smudged with a line of black and gray.

"So dusty!" she says, getting up. "And this morning I just swept and mopped!"

The front door opens. Mrs. Chandra looks up and sees Mr. Chandra wander in, shoes still on his feet.

"Ya, you know how it is," he is saying. "Darling, we're home! Oh."

So now Mr. Chandra has his arms up, as if he is trying to be friends with a tiger.

"Sorry, darling, sorry," he says. He backs away, out the door again – and he bumps into the smiling young man behind him.

"Hi, Mom!"

It is Mrs. Chandra's son. He has a girl with him: a Chinese girl, in long sleeves and a knee-length skirt.

"This is Sandy," Mrs. Chandra's son says.

"Hello, Auntie," the girl says.

"Hello, hello!" Mrs. Chandra says. "So nice, finally I get to meet you! Always Abhi is talking about you. Aiyo, such a pretty girl."

She puts a hand on the girl's cheek; the girl blushes. "Come in, come in," Mrs. Chandra says. "Sorry the floor is so dusty, why is because this uncle here always likes to wear his shoes into the house."

"I said sorry, isn't it?" Mr. Chandra says.

She'd cooked mutton curry and spicy potatoes, her son's favorites. As she clears the plates, she hears him pester Mr. Chandra to get one of those new smartphone things.

Her son is saying: "Look, look at this thing. It is a very useful thing! It looks at which roads are jammed, then it lets you know the fastest way to take. I use it every day coming back from work. And then: look, look at this thing. With this one, if you hear a song and you want to know what song it is, you turn this thing on, and you put it to the radio, and in a few seconds—"

"I don't need a new phone," Mr. Chandra says. "All these new things, you know they're not for me."

"As you can see, my parents are dinosaurs," her son says. His girlfriend giggles.

"As it is, having one phone is bad enough," Mr. Chandra says. "Last time all my friend's numbers I had memorized. Then I got this phone. Now, one number also I cannot remember!"

Her son says: "That's what your contact list is for, isn't it?"

Mr. Chandra says: "That! That's my point! You let your phone remember everything for you, do everything for you – when you don't have a phone, then how? Helpless!"

X

"One hundred times already I've said," Mr. Chandra says. "I don't need a new phone. These new things, you know they are not for me."

"You are such a dinosaur, Uncle!" her son's girlfriend says.

She is a white girl, her son's girlfriend. She wears a sleeveless blouse, and a pair of shorts – too short, so high up the thigh! And she has a big tattoo of a naked lady on her right shoulder, top to elbow. Even though it only shows the naked lady's back, still it's not decent.

Why does her son bring home girls like this?

Mrs. Chandra says: "Abhi, come help me with the dessert, please?"

Her son slouches into her kitchen. He is not smiling. He knows what helping her with the dessert means.

Through the door, at the dinner table, Mr. Chandra is saying: "You let your phone remember everything, do everything, but when you don't have a phone, how then? You'll be helpless. Like a chicken, no head!"

Her son's girlfriend laughs, "Ha-ha-ha!"

"What do you want, Mom?" her son says.

"I don't like her," Mrs. Chandra says. "What happened to the other one? The Chinese one. What was her name? I liked that one. She was very nice, I thought. Maybe nicer than this one, even. What was her name?"

"Sandy."

"Ya, Sandy, that one! Decent girl. This one, she has such a big tattoo. I know you young people like this kind of thing, but don't you think it is a bit shameful?"

"Okay, Mom," her son says. He is not smiling. He is not even looking at her now.

He turns around and leaves her in her kitchen. Outside he tells Mr. Chandra: "Dad, it's getting late actually, we're going to make a move."

"Oh baby, but we can stay," her son's white girlfriend says. "Your father is so funny!"

"She's humoring me."

"Uncle, I am totally not!" the girl says, touching his shoulder. "Ha-ha-ha!"

But in twenty minutes they are going. Her son and his girlfriend are hand-in-hand and they say goodnight to Mr. Chandra

– but her son ignores her. Mrs. Chandra is confused. Why did her son suddenly get angry? She was giving him gentle, mother-to-son advice only.

"I was giving him advice only," Mrs. Chandra says.

"Again you brought up the Sandy girl?" Mr. Chandra says, slamming the table. "Of course he got upset! What for did you go and do that, woman?"

Mrs. Chandra looks at him, afraid of his sudden outburst.

"What? Why you looking at me like that?" Mr. Chandra says. "You should know what you did wrong, isn't it? What, you mean to say – what? You don't remember what happened?"

X

"Mom, you really don't remember what happened?" her son asks her. "Are you serious?"

"Your Amma, she is going senile," Mr. Chandra says. "Again I tell her about it, again she forgets. Own son's business also cannot keep track."

"Not my fault, isn't it?" Mrs. Chandra says. "Who asked Abhi to have so many girlfriends?"

It is years ago now. Her son's Chinese girlfriend – Mrs. Chandra's favorite, the one she thought the most suitable – she turned out not to be that suitable, after all.

She was a bad girl. She was Abhi's girlfriend, but at the same time she had other boyfriends also. And then Abhi found out. He was so heartbroken he came back to live with his parents, for two weeks.

"For two weeks he didn't come out of his room!" Mr. Chandra says. "Just stayed in there, reading his old books. You were so worried! Every day you were knocking, knocking on his door: Abhi, want to talk? Are you okay? Come out, tell Amma what happened. Every day!"

"You wouldn't stop nagging me," her son says. He puts his arm around her, smiling; he kisses her on the cheek.

"Mom," he says. "You really can't remember? It might be serious. Seriously. You should go for check-up."

Mrs. Chandra says: "Aiyo, don't need to worry, I'm old. Being old is like this."

Though she is so very, very forgetful nowadays.

The usual thing is forgetting where she put her reading spectacles. And sometimes she mistakes weekends for weekdays. Sometimes she mistakes which days are days to go to temple.

Mrs. Chandra is reluctant to go to temple, nowadays. She worries. What if she goes, but she can't remember the names of people there? How to show her face, like that?

One morning she wanted to call Mr. Chandra, to remind him to buy soy sauce from the supermarket – but then she realized she didn't know his phone number; she couldn't remember it.

When Mr. Chandra got back to the house, he found his wife staring at the keypad of their telephone, on its stand by her dresser, crying quietly.

He put his arm around her and he kissed her.

"Darling, don't worry darling," he said. "It's not a big thing. I'll get you a phone, and done! Problem solved! No need to memorize numbers anymore; the phone does it for you. It can remember everything for you!"

X

In the morning Mrs. Chandra finds that they are out of soy sauce, and she wants to ask Mr. Chandra to buy a new bottle from Tan Brothers – but then she realizes she can't remember where she's put her phone.

She turns the house upside down looking for it.

Why is it so bad, her memory? How can it be? She is just sixty-plus.

Mr. Chandra's birthday: 27 June. Every two days he goes to the coffee shop to meet Dr. Rama and Mr. Netto, his cronies. The sports he follows in the newspaper: football, hockey, and – and one more? What is it?

Her son's favorite dishes: mutton curry, spiced potatoes. Her son's fiancée: they've been engaged for over a year already, and soon he will be getting married. Mrs. Chandra is happy about this. The girl, she is a good girl.

What is her name? Sandy?

Mrs. Chandra feels a little jealous of her son's fiancée. The young couple, they are young people: they get to do what they like. They go where they want to go. The two of them might be going to France to work.

No chance for her and Mr. Chandra to do those things any more. Go traveling-traveling abroad, and all. She is already fifty-plus. And with memory problems also.

Not all people have memory problems this bad, Mrs. Chandra thinks. It is unfair. Why is it so bad for her?

Looking up from her dressing table drawer and out the window, Mrs. Chandra notices a new supermarket down on the main road. It is a three-story building with billboards on every side.

Goat's Milk Body Lotion – for fairer, younger looking skin!
The Big Breakfast Burger Boss, only RM5.99!
Increase brainpower and do well in exams – drink Essence of Chicken!

Where did this supermarket come from?

Wasn't it a row of shophouses? What happened to – oh, yes. They tore down all the shophouses to make way for this supermarket, isn't it? Always it is extra dusty, because of the construction work. That's why nowadays she has to sweep and mop so often.

But when did they finish building the supermarket?

Mrs. Chandra shivers a little bit. She flings the curtains shut.

X

The Big Boss Burger Breakfast, only RM8.99!
Nutrex Sheep Placenta Extract – for fairer, younger looking skin!
Fortify your brainpower – drink Essence of Chicken, with added Ginseng!

Mrs. Chandra flings the curtains shut. Ever since they built that supermarket she has to sweep and mop every day. She goes down on her knees and wipes the floor with one finger, and it comes away smudged with gray and black.

"Look, how dusty!" she says.

She has to clean the house because her son and his fiancée are coming today; they are visiting from overseas.

The front door opens.

At first, Mrs. Chandra is angry: this man wanders in, reading his newspaper, still wearing his dirty sandals, stepping everywhere – so inconsiderate! But then she sees that the man is a stranger.

So she screams.

She gets up and runs up the staircase, and into the bedroom. She locks the door. She is panicking now. Who is this man? What does he want? Is he a robber? How did he get keys to the house?

Her heart races fast, and skips when the phone on her dresser rings. She snatches it.

"Eh, hello," Mr. Chandra says. "I got your soy sauce. What's wrong with you, woman? What for you suddenly run like—"

"Darling, please come home now darling," Mrs. Chandra says, whispering. "Please, there's a robber in the house."

"What?"

"A robber. How he got in, I don't know! Just only he came in the front door, I had to run upstairs. Please come home now!"

THE HUNGER HOUSES

RAYMOND G. FALGUI

The food appeared every night, but the squatters knew enough not to eat it.

Their homes were nothing but flattened cardboard boxes leaning against the vine-covered walls of the great houses, but those shacks had housed generation after generation of squatters, and they had learned the ways of the neighborhood much as their peasant forebears had learned the ways of the forest, field, and mountain. Their ancestors had learned to placate the aswang, the manananggal, the kapre; the descendants had learned to fear the may-ari, the owners of the houses.

Before the Second World War, the neighborhood had been the playground of Manila's elite. The great houses were like palaces, and like palaces they all seemed the same – each with its wide balconies, hanging gardens, and circular driveways. Now they were also similar in their ruin – the driveways overgrown with weeds, the gardens dead, the balconies empty. The families who lived in the great houses had died off or moved away; there was no one left to live in the great houses. But even decayed and abandoned, they were still not for the squatters.

The squatters first came to the city in great numbers after the war, when the breakdown of the old social order had allowed them to exchange the poverty of the country for the poverty of the city. None remained of the generation which first settled in the neighborhood, but they had passed on their hard-won lessons to their numerous descendants. And to those who doubted the lessons, who did not believe in the stories, there would always be a new arrival from the provinces or an ambitious squatter to provide an object lesson for the rest. A squatter would climb over the walls of one of the great houses, then open their gates to his kin. He would set his family up in one of the rooms of the great houses.

Nothing would happen for days, weeks, even a month, and the other squatters sweating or shivering in their shanties would look at the darkened house, noting the one room lighted by a kerosene lamp or warmed by a cooking fire.

"The foolish ones are still there," they would tell their children and each other.

"It is only a matter of time."

For the may-ari, the owners of the houses, were an impatient lot, and would not tolerate such insolence for long.

One night there would be screams, and on that night the squatters would shut themselves inside their claustrophobic shanties, refusing to look out.

The next night, the great houses would be darkened again, with not even a tiny candle to brighten a single room.

Thus the squatters learned to build their tenements alongside the walls of the great houses. The tenements grew so numerous that they seemed to be organic, a mold or fungus spreading along the walls.

But the squatters learned to leave the great houses themselves alone.

X

But the may-ari, the owners, were not content to merely protect their property. In life, they had been waited upon hand and foot, and they expected the same treatment to continue in the unlife.

So they left food outside the gates of the great houses.

No one saw who brought the food; it just appeared.

But the squatters knew if they ate the food, the may-ari, the owners, would own them as well.

"The owners of the houses are too selfish," the mothers told their children.

"Look at the houses. The owners are long gone, but still they will not let us use them. The owners prefer the houses stay empty than let us live in them.

"Look at the food, for it is given by the same, by those who give a little and take everything in return.

"If you eat even a little of the food, the owner will take you away, and we will never see you again."

So every night the squatters sent their children to beg in the streets – to tap on car windows for change or to chase foreigners stepping out of their hotels. They sent them to beg for they knew of nothing else to do with their children, but also to save them from the food of the great houses.

But there came a time when a new President of the Republic was elected, a man whose greatest achievement was to be born the son of an old President. Too late, Filipinos learned that rulership is not passed on like the shape of one's nose or the color of one's skin. For the son of the old President brought hard times down upon the country. Then the foreigners no longer came to visit, and the car windows did not roll down, for the pockets of the drivers were empty.

And so the beggar children of the squatters returned to their shanties tired and hungry, dreaming of the food of the great houses.

For one such child, dreaming was no longer enough.

One night, he did not return to his shanty, but stopped outside the gates of one of the great houses, and ate all the food he found there.

Then he laid himself down beside the gate and fell asleep looking at the stars, waiting for the may-ari to get him.

X

When he woke up, he thought he was still looking at the stars.

Then he realized the stars were actually candles, hundreds of them. He was in a room, lying on a bed. There were candles all over the room. He had never seen so many candles before. To have lighted that many candles in his shanty would have invited the walls to go up in flames.

A door opened.

He looked up, and saw Mang Domeng enter the room.

Mang Domeng had lived with his mother, but was not his father. Mang Domeng was the father of his two youngest brothers.

He expected to see Mang Domeng here. A week before, he had seen Mang Domeng take and eat a bit of cake from the same great house that he had chosen. Mang Domeng had eaten the cake, then had lain beside his mother to sleep. In the morning, Mang Domeng was gone.

"It is time to see the may-ari," Mang Domeng said.

He stood up from the bed, the only soft bed he had ever known, with reluctance.

He followed Mang Domeng down the lighted corridors into the heart of the house. But as he walked, he leaned his head to one side, listening. There was a whispering in the corridors, a whispering that came from the very walls of the great house.

Mang Domeng seemed to hear nothing.

He followed Mang Domeng into a large room, a room big enough to fit all the squatters of the neighborhood, and more.

The room was filled with pale men and women, whispering to each other, dancing, laughing, drinking, but not eating.

One of the pale men noticed Mang Domeng's arrival and left the others.

"I am the may-ari of this house," the pale man said, looking him over. "You can work on the upper floors, I think, cleaning and dusting.

"Take him away," the pale man told Mang Domeng, but he broke away from Mang Domeng's grasp and cheekily walked up to the pale man, who took a step back.

"Kakausapin ko ang may-ari ng bahay," he said. I want to talk to the owner of the house.

The speaking of the vernacular drew mixed reactions from the pale crowd.

"Que barbaridad," said one pale young woman, hiding her mouth with her fan.

"It's just the squatties," said a pale fat man. "We can't expect anything better of them, can we?"

The may-ari turned away, ignoring his request.

But he did not feel as he always did when, tapping at car windows, the drivers looked straight ahead, pretending he was not there. After a while, he started to think he was not there either.

This time was different. Perhaps it was because he had eaten his fill. Since he knew of the fate of Mang Domeng, who had been taken after eating the smallest bit of food, he had been determined to make the most of his meal. He had finished all the food before the gate – not a scrap or crumb remained. For the first time in his life, his stomach had growled in satisfaction, not in hunger.

And, perhaps, because he was not distracted by the hunger, he could hear the whispers.

And the whispers told him what to say.

"Kakausapin ko ang totoong may-ari ng bahay," he said. I want to talk to the true owner of the house.

The party fell silent.

"You dare?" the may-ari asked, turning back to look at him. The pale men and women looked on with interest. The owner of the house would make the dirty brown little boy pay for his insolence.

"You think to speak to the masters? Do you know Latin, or Sumerian, or Old Celtic? I studied Ancient Languages at the University of Barcelona, then at the University of Heidelberg.

"It was because of my knowledge of languages that I could read the old books Tito Morel brought with him after fleeing the Civil War in Spain. I read the old books, and I saw what had to be done.

"The coward McArthur had abandoned us. The buck-toothed Japanese wanted us to bow to them."

The pale men and women nodded their heads.

"But that was not the worst of it. The worst of it was the people we ruled over no longer obeyed. Your people no longer knew their place. Their place was to stay bound to the land, working the fields. If they came to the city, it would be at our behest: the men to work as drivers or gardeners, the women to serve as maids for our houses or as whores for the American soldiers.

"But your people came to the city, and stayed, and bred like rats."

The pale men and women nodded their heads.

"That was when I called to the Old Ones. I spoke to them using the dead languages. For language has always been our power, we have always spoken the language of those with power, whether Spaniards or Americans or Old Ones. For those with power share their power with us!"

The pale men and women nodded their heads.

"And the Old Ones understood! They heard my pleas! For they were here before the stars. They knew what it was to be usurped, to lose your place in the world.

"We offered them our hate, and the offering was accepted."

The pale men and women nodded their heads.

"We have always fed them well on our hatred," the pale man said. "What offering can you make?"

But he was not listening to the pale man; he was listening to the whispers, he was taking instruction from the true owners of the great house. He understood that the pale man was wrong, that the languages did not matter, that all that mattered was the need, that both may-ari and squatter possessed such a need, and that the squatter's need was stronger.

"Gutom," he said, answering the whispers, not the pale man. He told them of his need: Hunger.

"Take him away!" the pale man commanded, pointing at him with a long, smooth finger.

He ignored the shaking finger, still listening to the whispers. The Old Ones wanted blood, they wanted blood to seal the pact, and he knew where to get it.

Opening his mouth, he bit off the pale man's long finger.

The pale man screamed, and soon the pale men and women were screaming as well.

But he ignored them, savoring the taste as his teeth cracked finger bones. He had been full, but now he was getting hungry again.

"This is only one dirty brown little beggar boy!" the pale man shouted, trying to rally the others. One hand gripped the ruined one, trying to staunch the flow of blood.

"Our hate is still greater than his hunger!" the pale man shouted.

But he turned to Mang Domeng, who no longer looked at the pale man to tell him what to do.

"Buksan mo ang pintuan," he said. Open the doors.

"Nagugutom ang mga tao."

The people are hungry.

"Papasukin mo sila."

Let them in.

TRASH TALK

LYANA SHAH

I stopped talking in June. I made up my mind and that was that.

Have you ever stopped to wonder how long you can go without speaking? If you don't count eating or sleeping or working, it's not usually for very long, is it? If you're in a conversation with someone else, how long can you go before you feel the itch to tell a joke or complain about something? Try to be silent for once, just absolutely silent. Now, wait. How long do you think it will take for the other person to start squirming and asking, 'What's wrong?' and 'Why are you so quiet?'

Believe me, it won't be long.

It's something I've always given a lot of thought to. The amount of trash that comes out of people's mouths these days amazes me. If you sift out the small talk, the gossip and the niceties, there isn't much left of substance.

So I made the decision not to add to the bloated bubble of meaningless words polluting our world. My decision was like leaving one room, closing the door behind me, and entering a different room altogether. I was still the same deep down, but no one would believe that.

My friends at school were the first to notice. But I'm a quiet person, so it still took them three days to realize. My best friend Annie was more insistent than the others, asking if I was feeling ill – just because I hadn't said a word. I fished out my notebook and wrote: 'I'm fine. I just don't feel like talking.'

Although she looked a bit worried, she didn't press me further.

My friends wanted to know just how long I intended to 'not talk' for. A week? A month? A year? Out came the notebook again: 'For as long as I feel like it'.

Papa was next to notice my silence. He came to my room one evening and said, "We haven't talked in a while. How's school?"

I merely nodded. I'd sworn to never use my voice again. I would stick to my promise.

"OK. Uh ... have you had dinner?"

So much awkwardness. A nod. A smile. After seeing that he wasn't going to get any more from me, he left. And something in me eased slightly, like a tension I hadn't even known was there. Conversation was distraction. I found comfort in no longer playing along. I found comfort in my own thoughts, especially in memories of happier times.

The next day at school, I drew stares from my teacher during morning assembly. I think it was because I was not singing 'Majulah Singapura' with everyone else, but just standing there, staring at the flag. I studied the kids around me, who were mangling the words, snickering, and generally had no idea what in the world they were singing. It made me wonder why I was the one getting the stares, not them.

I was glad the teacher didn't confront me but, as it turned out, I was going to run into trouble soon.

"Mel," my English teacher called on me later that afternoon. It was the last class of the day. What a shame. I'd been so close to making it through the day undisturbed. I stopped doodling in my notebook and looked up.

"Why don't you read the next passage?"

She wanted to hear from me. They all wanted to hear from me. No ... that wasn't right. They didn't want to hear from me. They just wanted to hear *something*, anything, from anyone. Just to fill the silence. But I wanted to cling to that silence. It was safe – my own cocoon from the rest of the world.

I knew I couldn't just sit there. So I shifted. I pushed back my chair, its wooden legs scraping noisily in that tortured way they do. I stood up. I stared.

I liked my English teacher. She was smart as a whip, funny, and had an accent all her own, pieced together from living in various cities across the world: London, Bangkok, Tokyo, and now Singapore. I wanted to be like her. But I was just Mel, a girl who couldn't move forward anymore.

"Mel?" Mrs. De Souza prompted.

I did a slow blink.

"Well, what are you waiting for? Cat got your tongue?"

The class laughed. They were enjoying this. But she was growing annoyed, which was not in her nature. Does silence really have this power to change people?

"Mel," she said again, lower, more firmly. The fun Mrs. De Souza was fast disappearing, leaving behind only the teacher. The authority figure. The disciplinarian. But how does one discipline silence? Is silence submission or dissent?

"Pick up your book and *read the next passage*."

I picked up the English textbook, staring down at the jumbled words. The passage had something to do with a criminal getting caught and going to jail. For some reason, I felt like that criminal. I wanted to cry, but no tears would come, no matter how hard I tried.

Next to me, Annie raised her hand with a sigh. "Um, Mrs. De Souza, I think she's not feeling well."

Ah, the sickness card. It was a card I never played, but it might prove handy this time around.

Something softened in Mrs. De Souza's face. "Oh. Well, why didn't you just say so, Mel? Do you need to go see the school nurse?"

I shook my head adamantly.

"Are you sure?"

I switched to nodding.

"Well, OK, if you say so. School will be over soon, so why don't you just sit down and you can go home soon?"

Released from my impossible task, I sat down, and someone else was called to read instead – a tall, friendly-faced boy named Joe. Annie turned to me with a frown. "Mel, don't you think you're taking this a bit too far?"

I put my pencil to my notebook, scribbling furiously and underlining the words before showing it to her:

NO. I MADE A PROMISE.

She didn't say anything else, folding her arms over her chest. Now, my silence became hers.

X

On Saturday night, Papa took me out to dinner at a Japanese restaurant so we could spend some time together. I couldn't remember the last time we had done this. It was just the two of us now, and I felt guilty just for going out to have a fancy meal.

"This is nice," he commented, fiddling with everything on the table available for fiddling purposes: napkin, chopsticks, soy sauce.

I nodded a few times, staring at the menu. The waiter came – not Japanese, not even local, which I found ironic.

Papa ordered first – it was one of our unspoken rules. Then wordlessly, I pointed at what I wanted, while Papa's brows furrowed more and more.

"That's all?" the waiter asked. I nodded.

"Mel," Papa said disapprovingly at my rudeness, before turning to the young man. "I'm sorry."

The waiter smiled and answered in halting English. "No need to say sorry. I have a sister like her. Deaf since baby."

"Deaf??" Papa was stunned.

The waiter sauntered off, leaving Papa no room to say anything else. He turned to me. "What's wrong with you, Mel? Why are you not speaking?"

I laid my elbows on the table, lifting my shoulders in a shrug.

He gazed at me, pensive for the longest time. "Are you punishing me? Is that it?"

Not you, Papa. I shook my head, reaching out and laying my hand on his. He looked down sadly at my hand, then said: "I'm hoping ... that if we do happy things, maybe we can remember how. To be happy again, I mean."

He was trying. That was something at least. But I didn't believe it would work. Here we were while Mama was lying in a hospital bed, alive and yet not alive. I'd been keeping track of the days in my notebook – 118 days, or almost four months. Almost four months of not moving or eating or talking, just lying there, living through machines.

What about us left behind? A part of me was stuck with her on that hospital bed, trapped, waiting for what would come next. In my dreams, she was a tightrope walker, balancing high in the sky, and I was watching to see which side she would fall on: ours, or the side where we would never see her again.

X

My exams were coming up. I studied hard, because I knew it was what Mama would want. In my mind, I thought that maybe if I was a good student, a good daughter, she'd choose to come back to us instead of going to that other place.

The real problem cropped up when it came to my oral examinations. We laughed at them of course. They don't matter, we'd say. You'd have to be an idiot to fail. I called in sick on the day of my oral exam, but they just rescheduled it. There was no running from it.

This was like Mrs. De Souza all over again, I thought, as I approached the table and sat with the examiners. A passage to read. A picture to describe. The examiners looked at me, waiting. A man and a woman. The woman gave me a smile that was meant to be encouraging. She reminded me so much of Mama in that moment.

After a few seconds, I got up and turned around.

"Wait, where are you going?" the man asked. I didn't answer or so much as look back.

When Mrs. De Souza heard what had happened, she called Papa. He left work early to come down to the school and talk to her. They talked for almost an hour, while I waited in another room.

I imagined the things she was saying to him: *Something's wrong with her. I'm concerned. You need to get her professional help.*

More trash.

As I sat there, a few boys from my class walked by.

"Mel, heard you failed your oral!" one of them said to me, laughing. "Got a zero! A rotten egg!"

I wanted to tell him to shut up, but that would have meant speaking.

"Are you dumb?" another boy crowed. "What's wrong with you? Can't talk? Huh? Just move your lips and T-A-L-K lah! Not so difficult, right?"

They broke into laughter, until one of them – Joe – said, "Enough. Let's go." He looked at me apologetically before they left for soccer practice.

After they were gone, Papa emerged from the classroom, his face grave. "Mel," he greeted me tiredly. He looked at me, waiting for something, it seemed. Probably something that would prove Mrs. De Souza wrong.

Instead, I slipped off my chair, took his hand and nodded for us to go. I saw the way his shoulders deflated as he led me away.

The next day at school, someone passed me a note in class. I thought maybe it was from one of my friends, but that seemed unlikely because they now treated me as if I didn't exist. They allowed me to sit with them in assembly and recess, but I was just there. Invisible.

I opened the note. It said, 'Sorry those idiots bullied you. – Joe'

His handwriting was looped and a little messy. I wrote below it, 'It's OK. Thank you.' I passed the note back, but soon it came my way again.

'Good luck with your exams! Jiayou!'

He'd drawn a goofy smiling cat, and I couldn't help laughing. The sound drew Annie's attention, as well as my teacher's. Mr. Lee looked at me for a moment, blinking. "What's so funny, Mel?"

I shook my head a few times, looking away, and he ignored me and resumed writing on the whiteboard.

This was the first time Joe and I started passing notes, but not the last. We kept it up almost every day, sharing our thoughts, dreams and worries. I found out that he came from a big family, unlike me, and wanted to be a businessman when he grew up. I told him about my dream to travel the world. I told him about books I liked to read. But I didn't tell him about Mama. That was something I was not yet ready to face, much less share in a note.

X

In a city as noisy and fast-paced as Singapore, it's hard to find somewhere you can have a moment to yourself. A moment to think. A moment to cry.

It was nighttime, and I was sitting by a stretch of road, tears on my cheeks. The accident happened on a road just like this.

That accident put Mama to 'sleep', and when she wouldn't wake up, Papa did the unthinkable. He pushed her off the tightrope to the other side.

Mama was gone.

No more going shopping with her. No more rushing home to have dinner with her in front of our favorite TV serial. No more listening to her tell the story of the day I was born.

I had run out here after Papa came back from the hospital and told me what he'd done. I was angry ... or heartbroken ... or both. I couldn't be sure.

At least out here, I could finally hear myself think. More importantly, I believed Mama would be able to hear me think as well. I looked up into the night sky and told her that I loved her. I told her that I was sorry. I said goodbye to her.

Close to midnight, they found me. Not Papa, but a pair of police officers. I was exhausted from crying, so I got up and let them take me home.

Papa was furious, but I knew that his anger came from fear. Fear for what could have happened to me in those few hours when he didn't know where I was.

"She seems OK," one of the police officers said. "Just tired."

"She wouldn't say a word," the other police officer said.

"I know. She's like that. She ... hasn't been talking since we were in an accident a few months ago."

"Oh. Sorry to hear that, Sir. Please talk to her and make sure she doesn't run away like that again."

"I will."

The police officers left, and now it was just us. Papa sat me down in the living room, saying that he wanted to talk. Insisted on it. "If you don't want to talk, Mel, it's fine. Just listen. I need you to know that what I did today with your mother was the hardest thing I've ever done. I didn't want to do it, but I believe it was the right thing to do, and hopefully, one day, you will understand that."

I said nothing, pursing my lips tightly.

"I haven't sent you to see a counselor, even though your teacher advised me to, because I think it should be me who talks to you, not some stranger. And if you're not ready to talk to me yet, it's OK. I understand. I know why you stopped talking. Do you think I don't know? It wasn't your fault, Mel. It was an accident."

He remembered. He remembered my jabbering and laughing, my distracting Mama's attention in the car that night. The other car seemed to come from nowhere. There was no time to react. I remember the urgent blare of a car horn, exploding glass, and a scream that pierced the air and was cut short just as quickly.

"It was an accident," he said again.

An accident. He really believed that. He had let Mama go.

I observed his tired, bloodshot eyes, and saw pain in them. Pain that reflected my own.

"I hope she forgives me," he whispered, looking directly at me.

I hope she forgives us both, Papa.

X

'How, your marks?' It was a note from Joe after my exams.

'I failed my orals. But I got A's and B's in everything else,' I wrote back.

'Wah! Mine all C's. But never mind. So happy no more exams! Wanna celebrate? We go McDonalds, just you and me.'

'Really? But you know I don't talk.'

'Never mind lah. If you want, we can even Whatsapp at McDonald's. How?'

I thought a long time about that. You often see people sitting together in silence at restaurants because they're too busy texting. At least Joe and I would be texting each other.

I *did* want to go, so I looked up, caught Joe's eye from across the classroom and nodded. *Yes.*

Joe and I hung out at McDonald's for a few hours, where our entire conversation took the form of traded words, emoticons and funny videos we shared with each other. I felt that with time, I might be able to tell him about Mama. I liked to think Mama would like him. And maybe one day, I might even be ready to use my voice again and talk to Joe in person.

The next day, I was up early, earlier than Papa as always, and went about getting ready and making my own breakfast. But this time, before I left, I pulled out a Post-It note, wrote on it and pasted it on the fridge.

Good morning, Pa. — Love, Mel

Hopefully, it will be the first of many notes between us. Little notes, little pieces of trash to someone else, entire conversations to me.

Silence doesn't take us away from the world. Silence brings us closer to it. Silence lets us find the things we need, especially within ourselves.

As I headed out to go to school, I thought to myself that bad things may happen, but silence will always be my strength.

BABY'S BREATH

DIPIKA MUKHERJEE

It wasn't very clear to you, *exactly*, when the trouble started.

The photographs on the mantelpiece are arranged in chronological order, because your husband likes them just so. There's his kindergarten picture, hazy black-and-white faces in which you recognize him because he has claimed an image with an indelible finger smudge. Then the pictures of his family, his two brothers and four sisters, through the years in crisp collars and frilly frocks and tamped-back oil-slicked hair, later with bell-bottoms low on hips, and psychedelic shirts. A creamy birthday cake foregrounds the baby years; the teenagers pose back-to-back, like the Bay City Rollers. His parents, when present, always looked dour, his mother as chunky as the brick logo of the studio, Great Wall City on Batu Road in Kuala Lumpur, the logo sometimes the only spot of color. Then the wedding pictures, the four sisters married first, and finally the two brothers.

Your first appearance on this mantelpiece is with your head bowed as your husband ties the thali around your neck. Your face is indistinct, shiny, as if you may have been crying, but you weren't crying that day, not at all. You couldn't grin as widely as your husband – you were the bride after all – and the aunties were clucking about, commenting on how low your cleavage was, and how short the sleeves of your blouse, and the women on his side were openly appraising how light your wedding bangles seemed, how very cheap. But on that day you were struck dumb by the wonder of it all; of marrying a man so handsome, one who had a degree from MIT, and his family had all gone to college, a family so rich that they lived in a huge mansion in Damansara Heights, where you, miraculously, would also be living from this day onwards. You felt like the Gods themselves were showering marigold petals and rosewater on you as you took seven steps around the fire. Your fate had led you to this and you were most perfectly happy.

His home in Damansara Heights had a lot of rooms, but a lot of people too. Your mother-in-law did not approve of any of the doors being closed during the day. Besides your brother-in-law and his wife, there was always at least one sister's family in residence, due to marital or financial problems. You lay on your bed, dizzy from the frequent migraines, which grew worse after your marriage, and anyone in the house felt free to come in and inquire whether you had been throwing up, because of *good news*.

It became clear that you were expected to produce an heir, as soon as possible.

Outside the large electric security gates of this mansion were other women who were working in Malaysia; women who had been in school with you and now ran banks and NGOs and taught and healed, and had families too. The government was urging the Malays to have more children to bolster the Muslim majority of votes in the future, especially as the Chinese women seemed to have large broods of children. You were the tenth of thirteen surviving children and your parents seemed to have stopped registering the births after the sixth child. Your mother would allocate a new baby to the oldest sister, until it was time for that sister to be married. Your father had worked his whole life as a clerk with the Railways, Keretapi Tanah Melayu, and your childhood was spent in Brickfields, in cramped government quarters, with the jasmine and vada smells of fresh flowers and fried dough mingling in the narrow alleys. Your life, until your marriage, had been full of jostling people, in too-cramped spaces, where there was always someone cooking, and the smell of smog.

You were used to the babies in the house: your sisters' and your mother's, as well as the progeny of cousins and visiting relatives. But when you met your husband in the cool air-conditioned offices of an American oil company (where you were a secretary, and he was the new MIT-returned engineer) you thought your life would be about weekend getaways together and dinners for two. That's how he had courted you, for all those seven months, taking you first to Cameron Highlands, to feast on fresh cream and scones at the quaint old English Tudor house in the middle of the terraced tea estates, then, for four magical days, on the remote cabin on stilts on Pangkor Island, where you could have loud sex, which tested your boundaries in surprising ways, and no one could hear you except for the translucent white fish that came to lick your toes when you dipped into the sea, naked, at three o'clock in the morning. This was the life you had said *yes* to; actually, you would have said yes to an MIT-returned engineer even if he wasn't this perfect, but it was written on your forehead that you would marry this perfection and so you did.

It took you by surprise that you were expected to have a baby so soon. Even your husband started to say things like *Have one baby lah, just to shut them up, then can relax a bit.* You even tried to imagine having a baby as perfect as those on the tins of powdered milk, but your body lapsed into daily migraines which had you retching miserably into the toilet bowl, while the pregnancy tests remained resolutely negative.

You heard your sister-in-law whispering to a visiting relative about your hypochondria – *What to do, these low class people like that only, we have the same problem with the stupid maids.*

Your mother-in-law was a socialite who knew all the top doctors in town, so it was only the best gynaecologist for you, at Pantai Hospital, and he had to squeeze you in between a Datin and an MTV VJ who was about to marry into a royal family. During the car ride, your mother-in-law delicately patted her lips, and glancing once at the Malay driver, who had been driving her Jaguar for 12 years, she switched to Tamil from English and asked, *Ummm, does my son...know... what has to be done to you so that you get pregnant?*

You looked out of the window, your ears flaming in shame; to think she thought you so ignorant. You had finished school – perhaps if the quota system at the Malaysian universities had been more open to Indians, you would have even completed a bachelor's in History by now. So what if you didn't qualify for a bachelor's degree in Malaysia, you had completed a secretarial course, and bagged a job at a large multinational company where you had met her son ... and what about her son? you wanted to ask. The well-thumbed pornographic magazines were hidden in a cupboard below the winter clothes he had no occasion to use in Kuala Lumpur. You wanted to show her the stack of those pictures, some gummed together, some poses so unimaginable that you thought they had been photoshopped.

But you didn't say anything. You looked out the window and pretended not to hear while the old lady sucked air through her teeth in frustration.

The doctor at Pantai talked to your mother-in-law, explaining the tests. You were scheduled for multiple visits. After your marriage, you had given up your job; you understood how awkward it would have been to be the secretary of your husband's colleagues. You had thought about getting another job; with your new family's connections this would have been easy to do. The emails from overseas crowded your mailbox, from classmates who had been academically weaker, but whose parents could afford the tuition in Australia and Canada. Two of your Malay classmates were on government scholarships in America. You felt hollow inside, but reasoned that with your options, you had done very well for yourself. You secretly hoped that your husband would soon be transferred to the headquarters of his oil company in America, so that you could enroll at the University of Houston. You had already looked through the website online. You talked to your husband about Houston, but he was dismissive; although he didn't want to join the family business he didn't want to leave his family again either. He told you to keep busy in Kuala Lumpur, like the women in his family.

Then the migraines got worse, and the vomiting, and there were regular doctor's visits, and in a moment of clarity you realized that working was not what women in this family did. Your husband's sister-in-law, the one that lived in the same house, was an occasional aromatherapist, your mother-in-law was a women's activist who appeared regularly in iridescent saris on the pages of *What's On*, either holding huge bouquets of flowers, which dwarfed her, or giving out checks to a bowing recipient.

Your husband's sisters were mostly, when not plagued by their marital and financial woes, talking about starting a boutique in Bangsar in the near future.

You started to want a baby too – you willed it to happen – for the magic of a little being to make all your problems disappear, with a fairytale *pouf* of air. By then, the doctor had started shooting ink into your fallopian tubes to take pictures. The pain was excruciating. You had gotten used to the invasive prodding by nurses and interns and now your legs fell open easily, like a prostitute's limbs. You thought of cuddling a baby in your arms, and when even that wouldn't work your thoughts started growing dangerous: *Why doesn't anyone test him?*

You never voiced this thought, but you must have willed the doctor to hear it, for that's what he suggested. Your mother-in-law flapped about like a crazed chicken, outraged that there could be anything wrong in her family, after all she had birthed six children, and the other five of those children already had a child or two. She kept stressing that her *other* son was expecting the *second* child soon, as if it validated your husband's virility. Her sons, she shouted, had nothing wrong with them; both her sons were masculine enough to carry on the family name.

Your husband submitted ungraciously to the tests, telling you that he had, at MIT, sold his sperm by sitting in rooms with a magazine, but there was a time and an age for that. He made it sound as if it was your whim that led to this public humiliation. When the results came, and it turned out that your husband had low sperm motility, the doctor assured him it was nothing to worry about – maybe *that's* when the trouble started. The doctor went through the causes, all of which were treatable: elevated levels of zinc, hormonal imbalance, use of tobacco, and so on.

Although the use of alcohol could also cause a problem, your husband did not come home until the next morning, his breath reeking of whisky.

Everyone crept around the house on cat's feet, barely looking at you. When your husband woke up at noon and lumbered to the dining table, the voices became forced happy, your pregnant sister-in-law trilling a laugh which grated on your heart. They plied him with fresh orange juice and massaged his temples, but you refused to go near him.

You wanted to stop this humiliation that was threatening your marriage. That night, you first suggested adoption: How about a baby that looked like you both, from one of the orphanages in Malaysia, or even a newborn baby from India? That was the first time he hit you, slamming your face against the dresser, so that your lopsided face looked like you were sucking a sweet inside your right cheek for that whole week. He was immediately contrite and twisted himself like a snake at your feet, weeping on your toes, saying it would never happen again.

Your husband was traveling frequently by then, to the east coast of Malaysia, where the oil rigs drilled black gold into the Malaysian economy. He left for Terengganu the next day, even pecking you on the unbruised cheek in a public to show of apology. You felt like it was a new beginning, maybe things would get better from now on.

But a part of you knew that things had changed, irrevocably. There was the new smell in his hair, the way he started to grow a small beard, although you protested that it tickled your thighs unpleasantly. Once he came back from Terengganu with moon-shaped crescents on his skin, four distinct red marks. When you asked, he said that he had got caught in some thorny bushes when they had veered off the marked path to the rig. He described the big scratch on another engineer's arm, how they worried that it might turn septic in the tropical night.

You looked at his face, and smiled at his lies, powerless to do anything else. You quietly started to plot how to get away, from this, from him, and you told him you were thinking about learning how to drive. He agreed at once, telling you it was an excellent idea, anything to make you happy.

The family found you an instructor from a good Tamil family – after all there was all that time spent in a car alone, your hand below the Driving Instructor's on the gears, they wanted to be sure of the propriety of it all – and after three years you were suddenly out of the mansion, and on the roads of Kuala Lumpur, without any member of the family with you. The Driving Instructor was a 22 year old boy, he called you Elder Sister, *Akka* this, and *Akka* that, for two hours, three times a week. You felt intoxicated. You knew he was engaged to be married to a girl from Teluk Intan, it was an arranged marriage, so a little bit of harmless flirting seemed so delicious. Especially as your husband was away from the house more and more and came back as a stranger.

You didn't plan it to happen, but suddenly, the driving lessons involved going to dense tropical forest reserves where you discovered the joys of your body again. You took no precautions, thinking that if you did get pregnant, the child would look like your husband. It was thrilling to think that this was how it was done in Indian epics too, a barren queen going to a mystical sadhu, and hey presto, a child! The Driving Instructor and you got bolder, and his calling you *Akka* took on a husky sexiness that made you wet, even when you heard him on the phone. One day, while he was driving, you took him into your mouth. It took him by such surprise that he side-swiped a Sikh driver's taxi, taking the front fender right off and dragging it a few meters before both the cars could stop.

There was a truck driver leering at you from his height as he passed. You sank into the dust of the roadside, horrified by what you had become. The Driving Instructor spoke in rapid Hindi to the Sikh taxi driver – he watched a lot of Bollywood movies and was pretty good at groveling in the language – he even prostrated himself on the ground playfully to show how completely sorry he was. The Sikh driver let you both off quite easily, after collecting some money for repairs. Before he got into his taxi, the Sikh driver glanced at you as if you really were a worm, still squirming on the ground.

Of course word got around. You heard that your younger brother had gone with a bunch of boys to the Driving Instructor's house and roughed him up. You said the driving lessons made you panic, so you stopped. The wedding card was in the mail in two months, and even your husband came back for *that* wedding, forcing you to go in a peacock-blue sari with green tassels, weighted down by tons of the family gold, looking very wifely and traditional. The Driving Instructor looked splendid as a bridegroom, but as soon as he saw you he looked away. The bride from Teluk Intan (she looked like she was 18) clasped your hands in her own and breathed: *Thank you **so** much for coming Auntie, your blessings mean **so** much to us both.*

In one stroke, you became his auntie. You could hear someone softly tittering, and you felt old, tired by it all, especially as so many nights had passed without your husband's touch. In fact he hardly touched you now except to hurt you. It was as if the sight of you reignited his inner raging demon.

You started to explain away the bruises more and more creatively, losing track of what you had said to whom. One day, explaining to your brother (the same one who had roughed up the Driving Instructor) about how you had fallen off the banana boat on a recent trip to Thailand, you were interrupted by his hand on your arm and his gentle voice saying, *Akka, you've never been to Thailand.* And you saw your misery, as well as that unacceptable pity, mirrored in his eyes. This was your little brother, the only one who still lived at home with your sick mother (your father had passed away eight years earlier) and he was the only one who still seemed to care.

When your brother got into trouble, and was arrested, you were so detached from the outside world that you hadn't seen the signs. Your brother had joined the ten thousand Indian protestors, who, swelling to a mass of angry humanity, had gathered in temples that smelled of milk souring in the midday sun. The protestors, defying three days of official warnings, had finally mobilized the anger against the growing arrogance of a master race of Malays.

You watched the protest on TV, thousands of people, walking through downtown Kuala Lumpur as a pulsating human wave. A lone police car had pulled up onto the pavement, as if to make room for the swelling crowds. More people were coming from around Masjid Jamek and the LRT station, and you could see the Federal Reserve Unit and police cars amassed in that area. A group of men were coming down the road with a sky-blue banner, and the banner shivered in the wind.

You felt your heart tighten with premonition – the crowd looked like a sea of your relatives – *Where was your brother in this?*

The phone rang incessantly as you speed-dialed his number, but no one picked up at the other end. On the screen, you could see three men jump up onto a makeshift podium and wave Mahatma Gandhi's picture. A man with a megaphone started a speech in rapid Tamil, but was interrupted by passing protesters waving a banner **How Is Our Future Going To Be?** while chanting in loud voices. Then came the red fire trucks, rumbling in from a distance, the BOMBA lettering on the side clear in white. Red berets, black uniforms, red boots. Without any warning, the first canister whizzed toward the metro station with a plume of tear gas. There were distant screams, running hordes. The fire trucks aimed water jets spiked with chemicals at the panicked mass. The man holding a tall banner, protesting the destruction of Hindu temples, doubled-up in resistance to the jet, mooning the police, but he soon fell to the floor. Slogan-shouters were hurling water bottles and stones, then flower pots and shoes, at the advancing police before being beaten and dragged into police trucks. You could see hundreds of them, men and women, like little ants being drowned in a sea. Chants of *Hidup Rakyat* and *People Power* started up, then died down again.

When a niece called about your brother being in police custody, you called your husband immediately. He was in Penang that day, and although he said he would try to pull some strings, he was distracted on the phone. Your father-in-law made it clear that this was a problem of a certain class of delinquent, unemployed young men, and you should have nothing to do with them. Late in the night, your sister-in-law came into your bedroom and pleaded with you – your husband's brother was going to become a Datuk soon, he had certainly paid his dues – they didn't want you to do anything to compromise the family's future.

So you did not visit your brother before he was released.

You started to drink, only a little at first, to dull the pain, but it was never enough. Your husband was not at home anymore, and with you swaying around the house all day, the in-laws panicked. One day, there was a ticket for a pilgrimage to Tirupati on the dining table, just for you and your husband.

You wanted so much to believe. You wanted the sight of this great God to cure the unhappiness at the core of your being. When your husband promised to shave off all his hair in the ritual penance, you believed the miracle had already started. India's crowds, its smelly marketplaces, the long lines of sweaty people at the temple, made you feel sick, but you bore it all with a smile. The sight of Tirupati blinded you with all that gold and diamonds glittering among the flower garlands, for this was the richest Lord in all of India, and surely the most powerful. Your husband made his way to the Kalyana Katta and emerged with his head shaven. You were both abstaining from sex, meat and alcohol during the pilgrimage, and the heat blurred the days into a mass of inertness until it was time to go home to Kuala Lumpur.

It took only two months for your husband to come home raging and incoherent again. This time, he slapped your head against the wall before he even began to speak. You screamed. You could hear the huddled listeners outside the door, and a very gentle knock, and over it all you heard your husband cursing the Gods, pulling at the short strands of hair tufting his head, and moaning, yes moaning, that even this woman, the one that he had tonsured his head for so that he could finally have a son, had a miscarriage today. He had hoped so much. In his raging vomit it all came out; this young 19-year old who had a miscarriage today, the Chinese woman in Seremban, the Bidayuh woman in Sarawak...there were more, and all were infertile.

You knew he was seeing someone else – how could you not know? But for him to speak of it so openly, to speak of all the women he had been *fucking just for one single son* was unreal. You lay on the ground next to him, letting the blood seep through your hands. You thought of the young 19 year old woman, probably huddled all alone into a corner in the apartment in Ampang, probably bleeding a lot more than you.

The in-laws started to talk about adoption the next day. It would be easier and anonymous if you were to go to Sabah and get a child from there. They started working out the logistics of it all; the air travel, the hotel, the payments that would be made. They said your husband would prefer a son, and you snarled, yes, a son, for who would bring an accursed daughter into the world and want her to live your life?

It wasn't difficult to drink through the night, alone in your room, one bottle after another, until the room started to sway every time you raised your head. You forced yourself to drink another glass, then one more, then crawled out into the night. It was a moonless night, but the stars blinked luminously in the sky. You were burning up from a fire inside and you focused on that one light by the swimming pool, the only one that lit up the shallow blue water, only 4 feet deep. The guard was sleeping, but his dog lifted his head to look at you, then put his head on his paws again.

The water was far away and the breeze heavy with the fragrant quisqualis flowers unfurling pink and white. You puked, then forced yourself on, snakelike, to your blue oasis. There was a splash of water, the croak of a frog, then your gasp as you struggled to the surface. Your body grew heavier as you wondered if your husband was too well-connected to be held in custody for long.

You let your body surrender to the water despite the gasps for life, until you felt the peace of swimming in amniotic fluid.

You thought of how the family would hold a live chicken over your bloated face, the feet slashed exactly over your hair parting so that the blood would mark you as a married woman who had inauspiciously died. They would wrap you in the peacock blue silk sari you had worn for the Driving Instructor's wedding, then surround you on all sides with bouquets of lilies and roses and jasmine and marigolds, garish next to your grimace of death. Your husband would blubber to everyone how hard he had tried to save you, but it had been a matter of time. Your own family would come, a collection of sisters and brothers and nieces and cousins who would watch from the sidelines, too intimidated to participate.

Your body sank in the water, totally at peace.

Your brother would place a small white bouquet under your folded hands and walk away. Later the in-laws would say, *how cheap, real flowers also cannot lah, only filler stuff for bouquets, but what to expect from people of that class*, but that would be the only bouquet you would carry into the huge oven that would become your pyre. A small white popcorn of flowers which was the baby's breath.

You felt the fetal pull of another life, the swirling warm waters above your head, the maternal blood thrumming through your veins, then heard the shriek of an ambulance shattering the calm.

HOW TO MAKE WHITE PEOPLE HAPPY

TIMOTHY L. MARSH

Way over there on the Asian side of the Earth, on the saddles of two or three tectonic plates that buck like rodeo bulls every couple of months, sits the island republic of Indonesia – a shifting, fractured, shattered dish of a dominion with roughly 17,000 bits and pieces of itself spilled across the eastern equator. A lot of these pieces are unchartably small, some are quite large. A few are greatly inhabited, many are not; but all of them, regardless of size or population, share at least this one thing in common: they are all exceptionally poor, even the ones where white people go.

The most widely gallivanted of all these archipelagic morsels is by far the island of Bali – a destination famous round the world for its sumptuous resorts and shameless Anglo indulgence, significantly less famous for its native penury, and the home of a thousand other stories not much different from this one right here.

When I knew Ketut Sutapa he was 37-years-old with a rotten front tooth that never gave him any pain or stopped him from smiling. He was the definition of a self-made man, but constantly denied it because no man made himself without the help of God, and because it made other men in his village who weren't self-made a little sad and irritable.

Like a lot of Indonesians Ketut's life began with the kind of cards that couldn't easily beat a fold. At the age of 5 his widowed mother took him to the busiest road in Bali, gave him five packs of sticky rice wrapped in banana leaf, and deserted him. She stood on bended knee and told him without tears or memorable grief what she had to do and why: that the family was too poor and fatherless to care for so many children, that sooner or later someone would come along and give him a better life than she ever could, that this was a good road to be left on because white people with money used it all the time.

Two days later Ketut was picked up by the Salvation Army, fed, clothed, inoculated, sent to an orphanage and never adopted. The orphanage wasn't in the business of finding parents for its children; it was in the business of raising its children *like* a parent, then releasing them back into the poverty from which they'd been rescued.

Once, when Ketut was little, a beautiful white Australian couple appeared at the orphanage and spent a week taking several of the children for something like a test drive. The couple took Ketut for a walk on the beach and bought him a kiwi milkshake, and when it was all said and done took his best friend to Melbourne. "His hair was combed and mine wasn't," Ketut would always joke. "Now it's the first thing I do when I wake up."

At 18 the orphanage evicted Ketut via a work placement program that placed him as an apprentice cook at a 3-star resort for two US dollars a day, seven 13-hour Indonesian workdays a week. Within a year Ketut had vaulted from apprentice to master, and within another year he had mastered the entire cuisine of his culture. He cooked for all the tourists, and by and by learned enough English to teach other orphans how to say hello to white people and smile like Christmas morning so that their best friends wouldn't be taken to a better life instead of them, even if their hair wasn't combed.

The years were hard and boring and passed without occasion until one day when a bloated Dutchman checked-in to the resort.

The Dutchman was so rich and important that he'd never learned how to drive. He'd also never handled his own travel arrangements and had booked a 3-star resort by accident.

The Dutchman was inconsolable when he arrived at the resort and saw his crummy $400 villa without all the slightly more exorbitant luxuries of the $800 villas he was accustomed to, and ordered a heap of Indonesian food as a way of sulking. "Things can't get much worse," he sighed. He had reached a status in life where disappointment came with room service.

The Dutchman ordered several traditional dishes, like seafood nasi goreng and soto ayam. The dishes were a captivating new enjoyment, like Russian ballet dancing down every part of his pallet, and afterward he was so smitten by the performance that he stormed into the kitchen and demanded to meet the cook and take him back to his restaurant in Holland.

Ketut could hardly believe it. He was very excited and a little afraid.

He went out the next day and bought the nicest bag he could afford and some clothes to put in it. He'd never needed new clothes to put in a bag before, but he was going to the West, and in the West people carried things in bags like new clothes and sometimes nice watches and soaps.

He bought two shirts and a pair of slacks and immigrated to Leeuwarden to work for the Dutchman. The Dutchman gave Ketut a bicycle and a nice apartment, plus a big kitchen in his restaurant where Ketut created all kinds of simple rice dishes that customers called exotic and happily overpaid for.

The Dutchman was so pleased at how much everybody was overpaying at his restaurant that he offered to send Ketut to university just to keep him around for another four years. The plan worked perfectly until it came to an end. Four years later Ketut had a degree in hospitality management and enough money to come home and have children and actually keep those children.

The Dutchman was inconsolable. He offered Ketut anything he wanted to change his mind. He even learned to drive just to drive Ketut to the airport. "I've never driven or driven anyone to the airport in my life!" the Dutchman begged. "What do you say?"

"Ik wens jou veel geluk en voorspoed," Ketut said.

Along with English, he could now speak Dutch.

Ketut had departed Bali with one language and one bag of clothes. Now he was back with three of each plus some very nice soaps. He also had a nice watch.

The watch was German-made and kept the time in places like New York and Bogota. It looked very handsome but made other Balinese feel bad about themselves, so he didn't wear it. How would he like it if somebody tried to impress him?

Ketut went back to work at the same resort where the Dutchman had found him. The resort had grown two new stars since Ketut had been away. It had grown marble floors, bigger rooms, and an elite and premium style that included a 50-meter pool with several tinier pools around it. But most of all it had grown plenty of white people. The white people were like western vegetation that grew around the edges of the pool and swayed back and forth from one end of the resort to the other. They were very pretty and delicate and all the native staff worked and smiled hard to ensure their easy rock-a-bye remained at the resort and was free of aggravation.

One day Ketut was talking to one of the guests and mentioned that he'd gone to school in Europe. That afternoon he was called to the General Manager's office and told to take a seat.

The General Manager looked terribly serious, like maybe one of the guests had died from Ketut's cooking.

"Is there a problem?" Ketut asked. He wondered if the guest had an allergic reaction.

"Did you tell one of our guests that you went to school in Europe?" asked the General Manager.

"Yes," said Ketut. "I'm sorry."

"Did you tell them in English?" said the GM.

"I did," said Ketut. "I'm sorry."

"Is it true?" said the GM.

"It is," said Ketut. "I'm sorry."

"Congratulations," said the GM.

"Thank you," said Ketut. "For what?"

"You're my new assistant."

Ketut thought it was a joke. He could hardly believe it when he came to work the following morning and found a furnished office just for him. The office had a leather chair on wheels, and flowering plants, and an old Indonesian woman who wouldn't leave him alone until she made him coffee and watered the plants. Ketut liked everything except for the woman. The woman was like his German watch and made him feel bad whenever he saw her on the wrist of some menial duty he could've done himself.

At any rate, Ketut took on all the duties of Assistant Manager, and after a few weeks all the duties of General Manager, too. The General Manager had a problem. The problem had to do with prostitutes, but mostly it had to do with paying prostitutes with resort funds and sleeping with prostitutes in the presidential villa.

One day the General Manager didn't show up to work, and that afternoon Ketut was summoned to the owner's estate and told to take a seat beside the pool.

The owner looked terribly serious, as if someone had been paying for sex with his money.

"Did you know our General Manager was paying for prostitutes?" asked the owner.

"Yes," said Ketut. "I'm sorry."

"Did you know he was paying for them with resort funds?" said owner.

"No," said Ketut. "I'm sorry."

"Do *you* sleep with prostitutes?" said the owner.

"I don't," said Ketut. "I'm Christian."

"Congratulations," said the owner.

"Oh Lord," sighed Ketut. "For what?"

"You're the new GM."

Ketut had absolutely no desire for such a promotion because he was absolutely sure he'd screw it up. He pleaded with the owner to consider all the incompetence he'd bring to the position, but the owner was convinced that not paying prostitutes with his money was the direction his resort needed to go.

The next day Ketut became the interim General Manager of a 5-star Bali resort in Seminyak, and the next week the "interim" part withered off the title like a dead leaf that had never been on the right plant to begin with.

The resort flourished under Ketut's management. It didn't matter that he'd never quarterbacked a front office or controlled an F&B department, for he had mastered the most important knowledge a person in Bali could master: what white people liked.

He was seemingly so educated on the matter that banks and local businesses hired him for seminars to teach the great art of Anglo satisfaction. Ketut went to the seminars and got dozens of different questions all asking the same thing: How do you make white people happy?

Ketut had no idea how to make white people happy. It wasn't anything he'd ever worried about. But it was true that there was a lot of money to be made in doing so, and he felt obliged to offer the best answer he could. The answer usually went something like this:

"Good afternoon. My name is Ketut Sutapa and I am here today to talk about making westerners happy. I do not know what makes them happy all of the time, but I will tell you what happened with me and maybe that will mean something to you.

"When I was very little I had much less than any white person. I had almost nothing. I was left on a road and a group of white people took me from the road and gave me a home and some food. They did not ask me for money or work. They gave me these things even though I was little and dirty and could not give them anything in return. And that made them happy.

"But when I was older my teeth went bad and my hair wasn't nice, and that didn't make them happy. I was still dirty and poor, but they didn't like that anymore. I didn't see them for a long time. Then I grew up and learned their language and they were happy again. I learned how to cook the food of my people and they loved the food and gave me an education for it. They traded their education for my cooking. But when I got my education I took my cooking away and that made them unhappy again.

"So when I came home to Bali I went back to the kitchen to make them happy, but that made them the most unhappy of all. They didn't want their education cooking for them. They made me leave the kitchen and put me in charge of making them happy. I didn't do anything special. I talked to them nicely and smiled when they asked for things. And when they asked about my life I told them the truth, and they were happy. Almost grateful.

"In conclusion then: I speak to them in their language, I have less than almost any of them, and I smile when they ask for things. And that makes them happy. Thank you."

The audience almost always left Ketut's seminars looking for a refund. It didn't seem like he knew anything about white people. He might've known less than them.

Ketut didn't mind. He didn't know what white people wanted. He didn't care what they wanted. There was only one thing Ketut wanted, and that was to find his family, start a family, and keep a family happy and together.

He went back to the road where his mother had deserted him 30 years before. He wanted to find his original village and then locate his mother. He wanted to show her his diploma, which he kept folded neatly in his wallet, show her the fine paper it was printed on and the elegant European language that was printed upon it. He wanted to hold her hand and tell her things like:

"Now this family has money and can take care of itself. It does not have to leave its children by the road for rich foreigners to take them to better lives. It can give them those lives itself. And we will be proud and have nice soaps and raise our children under

God, because I can make people with money happy, and it will take us from nothing to anything."

Ketut searched all afternoon. Finally he found an old farmer who remembered his family, and even a little about him.

"You look different," the old man said.

"I'm not poor anymore," said Ketut.

The farmer led Ketut to his babyhood home, but it wasn't his home anymore. There were other poor babies and another poor mother there now. The mother had a grove of children and three jobs that had nothing to do with taking care of the children. She didn't know where Ketut's family was. She didn't know where the father of her children was. Two of her children had diarrhea. None of them had shoes. "Take this," Ketut said, and gave her a card with his name and number. Two days later her eldest son had a job at the hotel and was talking to white people.

That was as far as Ketut's story had come at the time that I knew him. He never went back to that road again, not even to drive on it. He made his money and ran his resort, and on nights when the kitchen was short-staffed he got behind the burners and worked his old magic with fervor and joy. He married a girl he'd met long ago at the orphanage and had three children, and he loved going to work because he loved providing for and coming home to children. His face had the life and youth of his children, and looking into it you could not detect any of the poverty or strain of obsequiousness that warps the spirits of so many others who are born into identical circumstance. Everything that could've been gained from the content of white people, he'd gained.

They'd made him happy.

CRUSH

RICHARD CALAYEG CORNELIO

I

Right until the Year of the Flood, we lived in a hundred-year-old house in the city center, a dusky affair with high, vaulted ceilings and walls made of real pine wood; eight drafty rooms upstairs that dripped history as it dropped slates; a grand staircase flanked by wooden balustrades and with dry, worn steps that still managed to hold out for years only because we had the fiddly science of shifting our weights down pat; and, my favorite part of the house, a spacious rooftop that looked out to the whole neighborhood, where I sneaked off to most afternoons dreaming of marrying our next-door neighbor, Mr. Isaac, till I wept in a fury of tears and defeat and everything turned carnation, mauve, pearl amethyst with the inexorable dusk.

The turn of the millennium was almost here, and doggedly I took stock of the years before I turned eighteen and worried day and night that the world would end before my love even realized he was madly, foolishly, rabidly, infinitely in love with me. I was sixteen and saw love as one would a hidden treasure buried deep in the seafloor, but I made no efforts at all at dredging up the treasure and fancied myself a princess to whom troves and bullions and king's ransoms came simply of their own accord.

Mr. Isaac was a tall, hollowly thin man who looked like he'd whittled away pounds in the name of scholarship, which was probably true, for he taught at the state university, was revered and liked by many, except perhaps when he wore his favorite green parka with a green beret, green pants, green pullover, and thankfully brown shoes – and, really, it was all you could do not to think of puke and not to torch to shreds all the sickeningly green stuff in his wardrobe. He'd only recently moved in from the States and I could distinctly recall the day he first stepped into the neighborhood, partly because it was a foggy night then and from out of the wafting whiteness he emerged, like an angel sent from heaven, and waved hello to me when he caught me peering down at him from the rooftop. But of course, I remembered it, for in those days we were made to believe that ghosts roamed the streets at night to steal strong-willed little girls away, and I hadn't known until then that ghosts had outrageously awful fashion sense.

My brother Jaypee liked to joke about and make a meal of my calf love every chance he got. Five years my junior, he was just being quite the airhead, nudging or poking me so violently in the side I almost fell off the curb when we passed by Mr. Isaac's, a turn-of-the century monstrosity, a door up the street from us, on the way home from school in the afternoons. If it was my lucky day, Mr. Isaac would be there in a wicker armchair on his screened porch, on his lap a heavy hardbound book, horn-rimmed glasses slipping a fraction down his nose. He squinted terribly, and Jaypee was forever and a day wagering our babies would for sure come out so squint-eyed, just like the father, that they couldn't tell a 'two' from a 'one', and sooner or later I'd need a pair of glasses too. The clown would double over with laughter, his eyes lighting up and crinkling till they looked like slits in his face, and my heart would crawl pounding out of my throat as Mr. Isaac looked up in wonder, saw us kids walking by and wished us a good afternoon. My gut turned so watery I thought I'd swoon.

A couple of times Jaypee wrestled off his clown shoes and, in some old fit of sobriety, asked me however I fell in love with a man probably half as old as Father. And so I told my brother about that one time I was on my nighttime walk, having stolen out of the house while Mother and Father plodded through the hills and valleys of slumber, the row of streetlights throwing down my shadow on the asphalt, turning everything the color of foil. Why I felt lonely then, I didn't now know, and the tears I remembered but didn't know what for.

I walked, then trotted, then ran across five blocks as the wind whipped against my face and wafted dry the tears spilling down my cheeks like runnels. I ran and, before I knew it, Brownie, the neighborhood dachshund, was drooling close on my heels, so I ran, ran for dear life, and who should I run slap into but Mr. Isaac of the horn-rimmed glasses, in a green dashiki upon whose misplaced patch pocket I cried, cried, wouldn't stop for all the world.

He walked me home under a cluster of stars peeking through a cloud-curtained, velvet sky. We heard the distant toll of church bells striking the witching hour of ghosts and night wanderers, of lovers and dreamers. Dead leaves littered the sidewalk. We walked in silence and gazed into the few houses still lit, paper lanterns flickering in the dead of the night.

At a street corner was a flame tree low enough for us, Jaypee and I, to swing on its branches till they snapped, back when we were kids and goosey, and whose crusted bark we'd peeled off with penknives or forks in the dopey hope of making a pasty aspartame. Now it was strung aglitter with capiz lamps, like moths of paper spun from fire. And through the leaves I saw Mrs. Espino in a lonely corner of her parlor, reading by the measly light of a gooseneck lamp, hunched over a magazine like a question mark. Upon the dusted mantelpiece was perched the framed photo of her husband, who had a year ago headed for the hills.

"Why?" asked Mr. Isaac, and I told him how the Espinos had let in a couple of outsiders and fed them for well over nine months, before the Lopezes from across them found out and informed the constabulary on them.

Then the two of us walked on, alone with our thoughts, passing Bermuda lawns and dark porches. The moon-silvered path gave way to a rustling carpet of fallen leaves under the dappled shade of a sprawling weeping willow. Finally, he broke the silence and told me of some faraway place where people were free to leave the city, free to choose who they wished to rule them, free to live, free to love – and it was all too good to be true; like walking into an enchanted land of glittering trees and gold-paved paths and irresistible cherubs giggling behind billowy white clouds.

There was in the air the strong scent of calachuchi. I liked to imagine that he stopped in his tracks and broke off a stem of the flower to loop behind my ear, under a tracery of bowery boughs that made for a cathedral and the moon that made for a chandelier. But the clouds had blotted out the moon, our steps growing fretful and wearied, and we just walked on in comfortable silence. I'd walked this street many times, knew by heart where the sewer grating was, into which I'd dropped in my haste and frivolous inattention perhaps a hundred peso coins, now sludge-caked, lost forever. I knew the old, old man, though not by name, who owned the only brownstone in our village, and yet spent nights slumped by the post that held our street sign, hissing and muttering and wheezing. I knew the lady with a bottom half heavier than the top, who, every night she took her rust-colored mutt out for a jaunt round the block, seemed to glide instead of walk. I knew she talked to the dog during these walks, but I doubted it had the willing ears to share her sorrows. I knew the Mendozas sent their son to a boarding school abroad and that the Abads never liked long hair but wanted to save on monthly haircuts, and that the Villanuevas weren't agnostics at all but simply disdained giving oblations to the church. And I knew that in a heartbeat I'd hear not the trees rustling against the wind, nor the soft swish of my jammies, nor the rise and fall of his breathing beside me, but rather the persistent thuds my heart perched in my throat made, threatening to spill over.

And that was how I knew, with the certainty of all prophets, that I'd already lost my heart.

Every hush between a breath and the beginning of the next was infinite, full of possibilities, and I treasured each as we shuffled our way to our front yard. I found it incredible that only forty-five minutes had passed since I'd rammed into him, for it seemed to me forever. The night breeze hit my bare, thin arms and I felt like hugging him, as if he were a post and I might be blown away. I walked up our front steps, thanked him, meekly, wished him a good night, and we both retreated into the shadows with the knowledge that tonight was all the beginning of everything and nothing.

II

Hours of summertime found me up on my rooftop, surrounded by books I'd checked out from the library, and there I looked over at my old schoolyard and whispered a farewell heard only by oblivious gods. I wanted to leave the featherbedded life I had in the village, to explore the city beyond green lawns and ballparks, and this longing I felt as I leaned over the railings ringing the roof and wanted more than anything to grow wings, fling myself down, and sweep scythe-like through the clouds, like an eagle testing its halters and pinions for the first time. But I didn't need to wait long, for in a month I was boarding the train, zipping through the city to get to a university kilometers away from home.

In the meantime, my mother, as you'd expect of a woman who puttered bristling with mops and brooms around the house, subjected me to endless lessons of embroidery, laundering, cooking. Now, Mother was *the* perfect mother – never would you light upon a breadcrumb on the lacquered table, a spot in the kitchen, a stubborn stain on the tablecloth, a coffee ring on the broadloom rugs, a mismatched button in my Sunday dresses, a fallen eyelash on her perpetually floury face or a twig stuck in her shiny bouffant hair.

One time, upon seeing the row of drawings tacked on my bedroom wall, she told me it would be really better next time if I colored inside the lines, but I never yielded and she was almost close to tears when she saw my next batch of sketches, ghastlier than the first, with the Cray-Pas straddling defiantly the penciled lines. All the time Mother was nearly apoplectic.

Ah, I was a lost cause. Several times, I almost sewed my finger into the embroidery hoop I was sticking my needle in and out of, and another time I burned my right wrist against a scorching skillet and doltishly dropped the pot cover which shielded me against the sizzling slobber of the milkfish I was frying. I sang so off-key, thunderclouds brooded over the neighborhood and might spark lightning at any moment. I danced like a cockroach shimmying to some epileptic beat. I sat harum-scarum, scratched my thighs repeatedly, for my petticoat was itchy and miserable to move around in. My hair was a hornet's nest, and so many sucking lice spawned eggs in it that Mother nearly singed it all off in frustration. It came to a point where I feared Mother had asthma, for every time I picked up a needle or yarn I could hear her breathing heavily through her nose, muttering prayers.

"How can Mr. Isaac love you," taunted Jaypee, "when you can't even do a simple hemstitch?"

But in those sweltering days Mr. Isaac hardly crossed my mind. Our high school valedictorian had confessed his love for me, and for weeks I delighted in baking dry, bricklike coffee rolls he'd dumbly scarf down, blue in the face, and in bossing him around. Rogel was stocky and sprang up and down on the balls of his feet when walking to keep up with me, for I was at least six inches taller and had legs miles long. Yet, to his dismay, I never slouched around just so he'd feel tall. Together, we strolled around like mother and son in the afternoons, during which time I had to listen to his incoherent litanies how siphons worked, about air pressure and the law of conservation of energy and gravity governing the rise and fall of bodies. But it was summer and all around me were chain-link fences; how I wanted to break through them all. During his stump speech one late afternoon I cut in on him and talked about a faraway place where people were free to leave the city, free to explore the world outside, and all the while Rogel, mouth agape, looked at me as if for the first time.

That was how things ended between us, and if it was my reward for tormenting him then there was something to say for sin after all. I'd considered talking to Father about boys, but quickly dismissed the idea as he was in over his head already about the rumored recent trespass of outsiders, who had left behind a human flotsam of sleeping bags and broadsheet pages they must have slept under, in front of the church. People promptly went to the pound and took home pit bulls, frothing at the mouth, ready to pounce on and maul to death the unsuspecting outsiders, if it came to that.

There was also the smell that had been bothering the entire neighborhood. We'd suspected it issued from the Dizons' kitchen, where every Friday they cooked daing and tuyo, but who smugly denied such a thing and insisted it was some exotic species of red salmon from the Mediterranean. The oppressive stench hung like a thick, stale fog in the air. It got into everything, into our clothes and our hair, as if it were just wagging its tail right under our nose. When the wind picked up, the air seemed to drift with its tendrils reaching into every window and clinging to the drapes and couches and jumping right in the shower with you.

It was too much, and one day my mother came up with one of the prize statements of hers, which made you want to either throw yourself in front of an oncoming train or flush your head down the toilet.

"This is the smell of our sins," she declared, and suddenly I felt guilty to death, and on my knees prayed three Hail Mary's to atone for my sins.

Five airplanes swooped dangerously low over us, one morning. They rained upon us drops of lavender-smelling water that lasted for quite a while. The long-parched earth breathed lavender, and we went about the village smiling and sniffing like crazy dogs. It was on one of these afternoons that I caught sight of one encyclopedia I'd long ago forgotten I owned, its dog-eared pages peeking through the latticework to our crawl space. Jaypee, when I told him this, let me in on his discovery of a knothole in the mango tree in our backyard. It contained, among other things, rolls of thread and a plump pumpkin pincushion which, I recalled, miraculously disappeared from my sewing box. I knew Jaypee had already put two and two together, for though he was plain silly most of the time, he was still my little clever brother who once made a hair-dryer out of a mixing bowl and a smoothing iron, never mind it had burned my scalp for one minute and nearly electrocuted the living daylights out of me.

It remained our secret. A look passed between Jaypee and me over dinner when my mother complained of missing tomatoes and even kaning baboy, and the three gold-rimmed plates exported from Germany just a year before, that unexpectedly she'd found near the garbage pail out back. We'd decided, too, not to let whoever was sheltering in our crawl space know that we knew. Dolorously, I'd go to school every morning and in the shadows of my mother's shrubbery I could almost believe there were eyes regarding me, stealthily, and I let them.

Classes had started out pretty grim anyway, and even inside the classroom my mind would float far beyond the eight-hundred-foot walls hemming us in, and wonder what it was about outside that made some people there encroach on our city. My professors were beldams who scowled down at us with the kind of murderous frowns that could freeze to death a flock of birds mid-flight, and always one of them, Mrs. Prieto of dressmaking thrice a week, would catch me mooning around and shower upon me the wrath of gods. Sighing, I'd run up away with my fancy sequins and balls of yarn and tambours, needles gleaming silvery in the sun.

The state university was far from what I'd imagined. The libraries, worse than our village's, only allowed girls in if they were given an instructor's permit. It had been almost two months into the semester before I mastered at last Mrs. De Castro's signature, which resembled less a humanly scrawl and more a doodle of a three-year-old rabbit if it were taught writing. But there, in between shelves and shelves of books, I never read up on whipstitching or how to make truffles or bonbons. Endlessly, I read about the rise and decline of nations, structures of power and systems of oppression, till my head felt so full and overripe it might snap from my neck any second. I was dizzy with facts. At dinner I'd try to conceal the blush creeping up my cheeks, the twinkle in my eyes, by tucking in my shoulders and feigning boredom. But Jaypee knew me so well, and would say, in a slightly amused tone, "Look at Theresa, Mama, Papa! She looks like she's finally kissed Mr. Isaac!"

And yet Jaypee's words wouldn't be true until the last week of the semester, when, as a sub, Prof. Isaac supervised the freshmen's field trip somewhere outside the city, as was school tradition.

By this time I was almost seventeen and had gotten over my infatuation with our next-door neighbor. I passed him in the hallways and felt not a single flutter of butterflies in the knots of my gut. He was still the tall, hollowly thin man I'd first fell in love with, the man who loved the color green and wore horn-rimmed glasses. I remembered nights up on my rooftop fantasizing scenarios with which our walk that one cold night outside, me in my nightshirt and pajamas, he in a dashiki and faded cutoffs, could've ended differently. I'd conjured moments from that encounter to a place he told me about, some faraway, perhaps otherworldly land of glittering trees and people blissfully basking in freedom. And these thoughts whirled in my head on our field trip, as the bus shuddered, hurtled forward, into an unnerving tunnel-like darkness, then into a glare of light, out of the city.

Outside was the city in a shambles. Out the bus windows, we saw men and women walking around on the street – dejectedly. It was a blur of charred buildings and pitched collapsible shelters, belly-down splay of topless men and children in sewage lakes.

At some corner the shuttle dislodged us, and so hesitantly we stepped off onto the rutted street. Mr. Isaac took the lead. There was the reek we knew all too well that now assailed our noses, coming from everywhere. We walked a long time. We watched kids no taller than my waist carry to and fro buckets of water and scurry after cigarette packets tossed on the sidewalks, which abruptly fell off to give way to filth and mucky pools of gray water.

I glanced that way, saw five naked children, dongs dangling and fannies flashing, bickering over a can of water from a sawn-off drum, others screaming and running freely after skeletal dogs through treacherous alleys and winding side streets. And when I glanced this way, I saw houses stacked upon one another, cobbled together with tarpaulins, canvas, corrugated tin, wood, rusting iron, jutting out, caving in, pitching to the left, toppling over to the right.

Under a scraggly tree, a frail, old woman was peddling to us her banana cues and turon swarmed by buzzing flies, in a feeble, world-weary voice. Grinning shrimpy kids followed us down the rocky streets. We walked along shanties and saw yet more garbage strewn around, and I felt sick to my stomach. All along the way curious faces peered around doors, through broken holes of windows, wanting.

Many of us, in our pristine dresses and polished shoes, slumped over a gutter and retched. A group of women in flimsy dusters scowled at us, for down the road flowed a rivulet of our vomit, reminders of what sumptuous meals we'd had for lunch, mixing with the white soap suds of their laundry, with piss and mud. We were crying. We were guilty. I craned my neck up, wished I hadn't. Overshadowing the street was a mountain of trash frantic with rats. Pickers smeared their elbows and knees climbing the slope with crooked two-foot poles, indifferent to the stench cloud crowning the summit. A child squatting on the edge of a cliff, a sheer drop from death, wasn't about to jump off but was only defecating for all the world to see. Grimacing, he wagged his flyspeck prick at us.

The smoky mountains sprawled like a slumbering giant all around, as though walling away the city's high concrete borders. Through the crack between the mountains ran a river the color of carbon black. A trio of girls dressed in filthy ragged clothes combed the water's surface with their fingers. One of them picked up a rock under the meager palm fronds, skimmed it in an arc across the river.

Beside me, my classmate, a girl who coiffured her long, silky hair for six hours, was nibbling the ends of her braid as if to muffle her cry. I looked over at Mr. Isaac who stood a little apart from us, his face contorted with what I guessed was sadness. A girl trudged by, heavy jute-sack bag slung over her shoulder, barefoot, the scabs on her knees sucked on by flies and malarial mosquitoes. We walked on in muted horror, over potholes and dried, crumbled dog turds, past hummocks of refuse, blood-stained tampons, broken whiskey bottles, balled-up soiled clothes, umbrellas stripped to the ribs by some typhoon, papers, stinking leftover meals and excesses, sailing crazily along the gutter.

And then it was over. We filed into the bus, shaken. We were too weak to speak, let alone move in our pillow-ticking seats. Relieved, we breathed in the stuffy, frigid air inside. We groaned when the bus made as if it were stuck in the muddy road, but a heartbeat later it hissed and moved forward. I looked out the window and saw a woman pocked with ghastly open sores, her eyes glued shut by dirt, by pus, in her arms a baby, who seemed dead but for the jerk of its arms, reaching out. I reached up as if to clutch the air. Then I turned away, closing my eyes with an almost physical pain.

But I had no sooner made forty winks than I bolted awake at a tentative tap on my arm. In front of me, bent on his knee, was Mr. Isaac. All around us were empty seats, and out the window I saw the familiar tree-lined avenue of the campus grounds. Somehow the sun had slinked off onto the horizon, behind treetops, and I had in my sleep kicked off my shoes, now nowhere to be found.

It wasn't the first time I walked shivering and barefoot on asphalt in the deepening twilight, but it was the first time I did so with someone beside me. Mr. Isaac and I passed under a row of streetlights, our shadows gamboling on behind us. "How old do you think are these trees?" His voice interrupted my thoughts. "They've been here forever," I said, "Older than we are."

In the cool linger of the night they took on a deathless look and I knew at once they'd be here, their roots firmly planted in the soil, long after I'd kicked the bucket and been fodder for creepy-crawlies that would pamper the earth for another rambling copse of trees and wilderness. Overhead was a thick canopy of leaves formed by branches twining themselves together as if for comfort, and I looked down at the intricate curlicue shadows they impressed on the asphalt, like tea leaves boding a future both unmapped and untrammeled. I told him this.

"But they don't matter," he said, his eyes sparkling. "Because shadows occupy space but don't have mass."

I smiled at his lame attempt at humor.

"Why?" I asked, and he and I both knew what I was pertaining to.

"I want you to know what's out there."

"What for?"

"So you'll know at whose expense you're enjoying all your privileges now. All your freedom."

"But I'm not happy. I'm not free. Far from it."

"We're all born unhappy."

"We were hosting outsiders under our house, did you know?"

"Really?"

"Yes, they're a family of three. I saw the child one night. She was six, seven, I don't know. I saw her bent over a book I'd dumped many months ago. She was crying for some reason, and so I walked up to her and threw my arms around her. In a minute we were both crying like crazy. We only broke apart when we heard someone cough behind us. It was the mother, I think. I ran into the house. The next morning I peered into our crawl space and saw nobody. Like they were never even real.

"Theresa—"

His breath rasped the wind and bit off the end of my name. I felt cold. I rubbed my palms together and pressed them to my cheeks. I walked ahead of him and saw by the rusty gate swinging crookedly on squeaky hinges a trash can knocked over.

Trash, I thought, *it's following me around.*

The plastic bag inside was split open, unraveling crumpled papers, cigarette butts, plastic pull tabs, used coffee cups that bled shamelessly onto the sidewalk. The dented lid was thrown halfway across the grass, and I was about to pick it up when from behind me Mr. Isaac gripped my arm, wheeled me around and kissed me lightly on the lips. I could feel my heart had leapt to my throat, because everything was just all too perfect in such an imperfect world. I pressed my hand on his face and it came away wet. Sobbing, he took my hand, and kissed it to his lips, held on to it for a long moment.

III

Early in the evening of the day the walls were toppled, our neighborhood became a great blue void, dotted by arms flailing and heads breaking through the surface like ants swimming in a child's glass of water. The pillar-like trees were swept by so fast that they came off the earth in a tangle of roots and branches.

We'd scaled the slope of my roof and stood on its beaten shingles surveying what remained of the city. Houses were crushed in the rage of water as black as the sky, which for months had emptied on us a deluge so unappeasable in its fury, to drown the guilty and innocent alike.

As if they were only a pyramid of cards, or houses made out of matchsticks, buildings and telephone lines detached from the ground with a sound I'd never forget – *Krr-r-ssh* – until they tipped and sprawled defeated under the filthy surf. We saw all manner of things afloat in the water: splinters of wood, pieces of plastic, felled trees, rafters, roofs of houses, dead bodies, my brother; and, really, among the remnants of our vanquished lives, how could we differentiate at all what was trash and was not?

It was only four nights later when we saw the moon peek through the sky, dim at first, then bright and clear, full of promise. It smiled at me and there was a feeling of peace in the air. I leaned over the battered railings of my rooftop, in my sundress drenched, and felt the air heave the smell in from the water below. It seemed only a minute ago that I dreamed to grow wings and soar afloat in the sky, but now the black naked sea beneath looked inviting. One single step toward the void, one single step to cease all the desires that attended living. I saw my body below. I held my breath.

AND THE HEAVENS YOUR CANOPY

TED MAHSUN

The communal announcement from the Secular Authorities blared over the speakers and echoed between the buildings: "Strictly no littering at all times. Perpetrators can be charged with the maximum penalty of eternal exile to the penal levels."

I never understood why the Secular Authorities took littering so seriously, especially when nobody had even so much as dropped a tissue in public in the last eighty years or so. Special recycling chutes were set up in every building and public space, and people knew to put them to proper use.

As usual, I tuned out the announcement and concentrated on calibrating windows. I couldn't see inside of course, because from where I stood all I could see was the dark carbon shade of the circuit board that coated the reverse side of the windows up there on level twenty, but even through the blaring din of the announcement I could hear a rhythmic tapping focused on the center of the panel closest to me. Someone inside was trying to reach out to me.

I sighed, placed my tools on the platform, and wiped the grease off my hands on the cloth around my neck. I reached out to the small access node and touched my finger on its sensor panel. The panel lit green, indicating it was ready to receive data. Using my neural processor, I gave it the sudo command to open the window.

The window popped open with a metallic gasp, then slid up, revealing the figure of a man looking anxiously back at me. He looked to be in his fifties, garbed in a blue-striped long-sleeved shirt, a brown pair of slacks, and wore a locater/partnering band on the fourth finger of his left hand. The band's blue light wasn't blinking.

I pulled the goggles up from my eyes so that they rested on my forehead. Then I gripped the guard rail on the platform and balanced my weight with my arms. "Yes?" I said, in a not-too-friendly tone. I needed to get back to work and these windows weren't going to recalibrate themselves.

The man looked behind him as if to make sure his room was truly empty of any other occupants, then peered out the window and took a look above and below him. Then he turned his attention back to me.

"Hey, miss," he said. "You the window cleaner?"

I tried not to roll my eyes.

"Window *programmer*," I said. "Yes, I am. How did you know I was here?"

"Oh, I switched the window view opacity to fifty percent so I could see what's going on outside as well."

"Well, it's just me out here," I said. "How can I help you, sir?"

"I, ah, I... can I ask you a question?" the man asked, rubbing his palms together.

"Sir, if you could just hurry it along..."

"Yes, yes, of course. I'm sorry. Look, a friend suggested I talk to you regarding the windows."

And here it came.

"Would it be possible if you could pull some strings, push some buttons and give an upgrade on my view subscription? I'm a little tired of seeing the same old skyscrapers, the same old buildings. You know, something other than the Petronas Twin Towers, the Menara KL, the Dayabumi, the Maybank Tower. I need to see something new when I look out of this office while I work. Think you could do something?"

"You mean..." I paused a short moment so that he would have a chance to rethink what he had actually requested of me. "You want free extra views?"

"If... if that would be all right," he stammered. "All right by *you*, I mean."

"It's *not* all right by me. It's illegal." I pulled the goggles back over my eyes. "Not too keen on having the Secular Authorities paying me a visit. Have a good day, sir." I reached for the access node.

"No, wait. Wait!" the man pleaded. "I might have something to offer you in return! Don't you want to know what I have?"

"Don't think so, sir. I get paid well enough for this job. Enough that I am happy not to accept bribes."

"Bribes? No, no, no. Who said anything about bribes? This is a gift..." He ran over to the desk in the middle of his office and swiped up a bright blue solidstate and waved it in my direction.

Even through the filtered lens of the goggles, I recognized the unique shade of blue. "Tickets to the Sky Dome," I said.

"That's right," the man said. "Ringgit can't buy everything. Only lottery winners get to view the sky."

"How do you know I want to view the sky?" I asked.

"Everybody wants to view the sky. Everybody. Even window cleaners."

"*Programmers*. Well, don't *you* want to view the sky?"

"I've already been. Wife won the last round and we went to see it together. This round it was me who won."

"Don't you want to go again? Doesn't your wife?"

The man cleared his throat and threw a quick glance at his locating/partnering band. "I, ah, I, well, I doubt she wants to again. I wouldn't want to go to the Sky Dome alone. So you can have these tickets instead. Go ahead and bring along a loved one or something."

I looked at the tickets. The date was for some time next month, the numbers flashed alluringly on the smooth blue surface. Lottery tickets were ridiculously ringgit-heavy to get ahold of. I'd always dreamed of viewing the sky from the Sky Dome, the only place in all the malls that was accessible for the public to enjoy the natural blueness of the actual sky.

Working as a window programmer who works on the side of skyscrapers meant that I never got to see anything other than other skyscrapers and of course that great climate controlling ceiling that covered the whole city, turning it into one mega city-spanning shopping mall which, in turn, was made by combining several other giant shopping malls. Always other buildings, never the real, actual sky.

"I couldn't possibly," I said.

The man shoved the blue wafer into my hand. "Sure you can. In return... well, my windows do need a subscription upgrade." He winked.

X

The next month I was scheduled to perform maintenance checks on the building with the windows where I had met the man who gave me the Sky Dome tickets. I reached the window where the man's office was located. Sure enough, there came the *tap-tapping* to signal me to open it.

I thumbed the access panel and the window gasped open once more.

"So? How was the—"

I motioned him to be quiet. I sudoed a disable command to my internal communications networks so my superiors wouldn't be able to eavesdrop on our conversation.

"It's okay to talk now," I said.

"Sorry, forgot about your comms. Anyway, just wanted to ask you how the Sky Dome was. You went last week right? Who was your plus one?"

"I brought along my andromaid."

"Your andromaid!" he said, throwing his arms in the air. "Aw! I told you to bring a loved one or something."

"Yes, and I brought *something*."

"Well, what did you think?"

"Think about what?"

"*Think about what?* The sky! What did you think about the sky!"

I didn't know what to say, so I told him the truth. "It was a little underwhelming."

"Underwhelming?" As I expected, he looked surprised, and even a little hurt, as if I had made a personal insult.

"I don't understand how such a splendid thing like the sky itself could be underwhelming!"

"Was it even the real sky? It didn't look real."

"Didn't look real? Of course it's real. You were on the very top of all the malls combined, the very peak of the city! How much more real can the sky get at that level?"

"I'm sorry, I didn't know you'd take this personally."

"Of course I'm taking this personally. Those were my tickets."

"Which you gave in exchange for new window views. Which, let me remind you, are illegal by the way. If ever the Secular Authorities find out your window is tuned to display a view of the Merlion Park—"

"Yeah, about that..."

"—without the proper permit and subscription they'd... wait. What? I gave you what you wanted, didn't I?"

"The new views you gave me," the man said, "didn't really captivate me as much as I thought they would."

"Why? What's wrong with them?"

"All those buildings, those vistas. I don't know. They just look fake."

I slammed my fist on the guard rail. "They don't! They're as real as they come. I programmed, modeled, textured, and shaded them myself! I can't believe you're saying they're fake."

"I can't believe you said the sky was fake."

"I said it *looked* fake."

We stood there, half way up the building, me on my window programmer's platform and him leaning out the window, glaring at each other. Eventually, he said, "Seems we've come to a stalemate."

"Yes." I sighed and shrugged. "Look, I'm sorry I hurt your feelings."

"It's okay. You really think the view of the sky in the Sky Dome looks fake? I mean, you're in the window business. You'd know. You think the Secular Authorities could've faked the whole thing?"

I gave some thought to it. The technology was definitely there. They could certainly simulate a window to the sky with the same kind of technology that we placed on our skyscrapers. It would have cost billions just because of the size and engineering involved to create the multiple curved panels for the Sky Dome, but sure, it was possible. "I suppose they could."

"Damn. How many more things do you think they're hiding from us? Do you think the sky even exists?"

My palms were clammy with sweat from gripping the guard rail too tight. So tight, my knuckles had lost their color. "You'd better watch what you're saying," I said. "Those words are clearly approaching sedition if you ask me. We're already in big enough trouble if they ever find out you have access to restricted, unapproved views. No need to add fuel to the fire!" I looked around. Nothing but the wind and other buildings and lots of windows up here. For now, at least.

"I suppose you're right," the man said. "Best you continue with your window work. Thanks for the... well, you know what."

"Yes, and thank you for the tickets."

X

It was a few weeks later when the subject of simulating skies in windows came up again, though this time from a surprising source. The rest of the crew were already on duty and had left. I held back; not wanting to get stuck in the rush when everybody else was leaving at the same time.

I was at the digital Kanban screen noting what needed to be done for the day when I noticed the notification panel blink red. A new memo had come in. I swiped it open and read: "Anyone good at sky modeling? Report to R&D Unit 12 immediately."

I scratched my head. Why would they want sky modelers? The R&D guys knew we just reused the shared assets if we needed a sky background. Most of the other window programmers just filled the background with more skyscrapers. To us lot, the skyscrapers *are* the sky.

I was curious about the memo though. I considered myself able to draw a cloud or two, and I often did in my spare time. I looked at all the tasks that needed to be done on the Kanban screen.

There were quite a lot.

I shrugged.

I suppose all those windows could wait a few more hours or so.

The elevator deposited me on the forty-fifth floor and I made my way down a stark white corridor lined with reinforced aluminum screens, which were at the moment set to opaque so that passersby would not be able to see what was going on inside the laboratories that occupied this floor. No one else was around, and the soundproofing must have been set to max, because all I could hear was the hum of the air-conditioning and my own controlled breathing.

The corridor took several turns as it followed the angles of the building. I kept on walking down the long corridor, hoping to see a sign or digital signal that would tell me where R&D Unit 12 was, but there were none. I passed several doors, but all of them were inaccessible, except for the last. The door lit green as I approached, and slid open. An andromaid, one of the newer models with a blank featureless globe upon its neck, stepped out. It stopped when it sensed me, but then quickly approached.

"Yes, are you lost?" the andromaid asked.

"I'm looking for R&D Unit 12," I said.

"I see. This is regarding the memo. Follow me."

The andromaid took me back through the door and I entered a large laboratory, filled with computers and instruments of all kinds, with monitors filled with streaming data covering all the walls. In the middle of the lab were tables with more instruments and miscellaneous electronics laid out on top. At the other end of the lab was a desk, stacked with strange slab-shaped items I couldn't recognize. As I approached I eyed them carefully because on the thinner sides were printed certain topics that piqued my interest.

Topics like, "The Art of Design", "Modeling 3D Architecture", "The Beauty of Landscaping" and other related subjects.

Behind the desk sat a bald man, hunched over, with skin wrinkled like a dried orange. Colored almost like one too. He looked up and saw me looking at the pile of items I didn't recognize.

"Ah, I see my books have gained your attention, kid," the man said.

I tried to restrain myself from showing surprise. They certainly did not look like any books I knew. They looked too fragile to store any kind of information in them.

"She's here regarding the memo," the andromaid said.

"Of course she is," the man snapped. "She wouldn't be here if I hadn't sent the memo. Wouldn't even been able to pass elevator security protocols."

"Yes, Dr. Munawar." The andromaid's globe for a head glowed pink, which slowly changed shade until it became red.

Dr. Munawar laughed. "You're a sensitive little thing, aren't you? Be off with you! Go do something useful for a change, rather than mope around every time I snark at you."

"Yes, Dr. Munawar." The andromaid slouched off, its globe now glowing positively crimson.

Once the andromaid had left the lab, Dr. Munawar turned his attention back to me. "No idea why they assigned one of those to my unit. Who the hell needs an andromaid that can have moods?" He shook his head.

I held out my hand. "Sir, hello. I'm—"

"Yes, yes, you're here because you think you can model skies," the man croaked. He stood up and walked around the desk toward me and wagged a finger. "Well, kid, I'll be the judge of that."

"I hope I can prove myself worthy of your standards, sir," I said.

"Show me some samples," Dr. Munawar said, pointing to an access node on one of the tables. I walked over and stamped my finger to the node. The monitors that lined the walls flashed, and the streams of data that had occupied them were replaced with my hours-long creative efforts at modeling realistic clouds in the sky. The fluffy digital clouds floated serenely against a brilliant cerulean sky. All of it of my making.

The man walked around the lab, hands behind his back. His eyes focused intently on the screens, studying my work, looking at every detail I had carved into those digital sculptures. After what seemed like forever, he shambled up to me and looked me in the eye. "Let me ask you something," he said, slowly, as if he was choosing his words carefully. "You've never seen the actual sky, have you? I mean the real sky, with your own eyes. Not from pictures or videos or 3D recreations made by other people."

"Of course I have," I said. "I just went to the Sky Dome last week."

The man's eyes widened and he grinned from ear to ear. "Interesting that you mention the Sky Dome! But we shall get back to that. For now, let's get to the matter at hand. You have never truly seen the sky."

"I apologize sir, but I did just say—"

"Yes, yes, I heard you. You went to the Sky Dome and you thought you saw the sky. But of course you haven't. Sometimes you sit in an enclosed space like this lab for so long, you tend to not notice the passage of time. I failed to realize how young you are. How young everybody else outside must be." He sighed.

"So it's true then, sir? The sky I saw at the Sky Dome was fake."

"You had your suspicions, eh? Observant, aren't you?"

"It's because I work with windows, sir. I know what makes a good model and what doesn't. And the clouds in the Sky Dome looked subpar at best."

The man scoffed. "Indeed. Yes, that echoes the feedback we've been getting. And so we come to the problem that has brought you here. We've had an increasing number of people complaining that the sky in the Sky Dome doesn't look real. Considering how difficult it is to get tickets, it's understandable they're upset."

"Why didn't you get some good modelers to do it before?" I asked. "Forgive me sir if I'm out of line, but you're only starting to worry about authenticity now?"

Dr. Munawar gave a resigned sigh and smiled at me. "You poor kid," he said. "Come on, let's go for a ride."

"May I ask where we're going, sir? I do need to get back to my duties. I've got a lot of windows to calibrate today."

"Oh, no need to worry about all that," Dr. Munawar said as he walked toward the door. "As of this moment, you've been reassigned to R&D Unit 12. You report directly to me now."

X

Dr. Munawar called up a trishaw and we took the tubular transport to a familiar place.

"The Sky Dome," I said, a bit flustered. "What are we doing here?"

"I'm going to show you something no one but a few select people have seen," Dr. Munawar said. "Come on, we'll go round the back. No need to go in through the front entrance. I hate it when the andromaid staff make a big deal when I show up."

We walked around the circular building until we reached an inconspicuous door. Dr. Munawar palmed the old-fashioned scanner by the side and the door slid open.

When we entered we found ourselves in a hall filled with desks and empty shelves, caked with dust. The lights were not activated by our presence and Dr. Munawar actually had to announce the word 'lights' before they came on. Even then they flickered slowly to life, buzzing loudly as they did. At the far end were windows – the old kind, the ones made with that fragile material, glass – that looked out onto nothing because a metal curtain was pulled down to block the view.

"What is this place?" I asked.

"Welcome to the old operations room of the Sky Dome. Before we had vat clones like you, before we had andromaids, everything had to be run manually and this was where it all happened. Of course, this was a very long time ago. Everything's automated now."

He led me to a corner of the hall where stairs led the way up. It felt weird at first climbing stairs that did not move, but it didn't take long to get used to it.

"These stairs wind around the Sky Dome building right up to the top," Dr. Munawar said. "There are about two hundred and seventy steps altogether. Are you up to the climb?"

"I think so," I said. "But are you?"

"Don't worry about me kid," he replied. "I got these replaced years ago." He tapped his legs and the metallic sound reverberated throughout the long stairway up.

Half an hour later we were at the top, and I was panting and heaving, my lungs scorched and tortured.

Dr. Munawar grinned. "Yes, it's usually the most difficult on the first climb. You'll get used to it in time. Here, drink some water."

When my lungs calmed down, I started to look around me, and the first thing I noticed was how much junk and litter there was strewn about. Obviously the Secular Authorities hadn't been up here in a while. If they had been they'd have thrown a fit. There was also something odd about the air. Didn't the climate control work up here? It was musty and there was a faint hint of something left to rot for a long time.

Then I noticed the one big thing that my new boss had wanted me to see all along. It was hard to miss because it was the biggest thing up there, looming as it did over me like a dark ominous shadow. It was in the shape of an overturned bowl, and covering its surface were massive arrays of electronics and machines, protected by thick, strong grilles. A discernible hum emanated from the electronics, occasionally punctuated with a buzz, or a crackle or two.

Slowly it dawned on me what the giant apparatus in front of me was.

"Welcome to the reverse side of the Sky Dome!" Dr. Munawar cried, his arms raised dramatically. "Something I am proud to announce I invented and have maintained these past years."

"The sky in the Sky Dome is simulated by all... *this*?" I waved toward the upside-down bowl.

Dr. Munawar laughed. "Yes! Look, I know they look massive in comparison to the window panes we now use to coat our buildings but this technology is close to being ninety years old now. It's the predecessor to the modern window pane.

"Back then we didn't even have proper 3D imaging panes. We had to simulate the sky using good old-fashioned techniques like parallax scrolling and transparent planes. Positively ancient compared to modern 3D modeling techniques.

"Unfortunately that meant the electronics required were too thick and unwieldy to enable us a proper depth of field realistic enough for people to actually believe that it was the real thing. It's a wonder we ever made it all work with the curvature of a dome, of all things."

"But why?" I asked. "Why go through all that effort just to show a simulated sky? Why didn't you just show the real sky?"

"Look up," Dr. Munawar said. "What do you see?"

"Nothing. It's the ceiling," I said. "It's the ceiling of this level, but the bottom of the first floor of the next mall above us. You could have just built the Sky Dome on the top-most mall where they can see the sky."

"Ah. Unfortunately, that's not the case at all," Dr. Munawar said, sighing. "Let me tell you a story. Long ago, several centuries ago now, there used to be a great city called Kuala Lumpur that existed under us. They produced more garbage than they could get rid of, and so before they were buried underneath it, they decided to shoot their garbage into outer space, despite the protestations of their neighbors. Meanwhile, space down on Earth was getting scarce, and so we built malls on top of malls on top of malls just to create more space for people to live and work in.

"Then, about a century later, the garbage began falling back to Earth, threatening to bury us underneath it again. This time it was worse because the garbage fell to Earth as fiery meteorites, posing considerable danger to our increasingly towering malls.

"It's funny, because there's this quote I like from an old book, long ago banned by the Secular Authorities of course. It goes like this: 'He Who made the Earth a resting-place for you and the heavens your canopy...'. It implies the sky is a canopy that protects us down here on Earth, and yet now it is the heavens themselves that pose the danger."

"Or to quote an old Malay proverb," I said, "we depend on the fence, but it is the fence that ends up eating the grain."

Dr. Munawar nodded. "You're more knowledgeable than I thought. So anyway, the Secular Authorities decided to build a great roof that covered the whole area to protect the malls and that's what you see above us right now. There's no more mall above us. This is the very top. And all this junk lying about? That's all garbage that fell from space before the roof was finished. You ever wondered why the Secular Authorities take littering extremely seriously? This is why."

"So the real sky has been blocked out for almost a century?" I asked. "Has anyone ever seen the sky since?"

"Not as far as I know," Dr. Munawar said. "I don't think anyone's gone to the other side in a long while."

"People still longed to see the sky," I said. "So you built the Sky Dome with the technology you had available. And given time, the people forgot that the sky wasn't even real."

Dr. Munawar nodded. "And in that time, the Secular Authorities learned that it was yet another weapon in their arsenal to control the masses. To control them by giving them another carrot to chase after."

"I suppose people didn't complain about the sky looking fake at the time because they knew the limitations of the technology then?"

"On the contrary, kid," Dr. Munawar said. "Me and my team were congratulated for creating such a realistic-looking sky. We actually recorded three-dimensional footage of the real sky before it was ultimately closed off forever and we used that to build the display that runs over the Sky Dome."

"You mean that's what the real sky actually looks like?" I said. "But it looks so... so unimpressive."

Dr. Munawar scoffed. "And therein lies the problem. You young kids are so desensitized to hyper-realistic imagery and visual stimulation that when you see the actual sky it looks plain and boring. Less than ordinary even. You need to see something flashy and bright."

The realization dawned upon me like a falling brick. "So you need me to rebuild the sky for a new generation. Something that's hyper-real. Something that's more real than real because it's what our generation is used to and what we have come to expect."

"Exactly," Dr. Munawar said. "I've resisted the calls to upgrade the sky footage on the Sky Dome for years but this year had the most complaints we've received so far. I was, let us say, compelled, to do something. And that something is getting you on board. It means losing what we have left of the real sky forever but that's not what people want anymore. I suppose it's time for me to let go."

X

I was having lunch in the plaza outside the Sky Dome, near the fountains which jetted classic plays, written by the twentieth century Malaysian playwright, Syed Alwi, in the form of spouting water.

The fountain was performing the second act of *Alang Rentak Seribu*, when I met him again.

"Hey, it's the window cleaner! It's so good to see you again. How are you doing?"

I looked up and saw the very same man who had stood at his window and asked me for illegal extra views. "Oh! What a pleasant surprise," I said. And it was. "It's window *programmer* by the way, though that's not really what I do anymore."

"That's right," he said. "I haven't seen you at the windows in a while. What have you been up to?"

"I've been transferred elsewhere. Doing something much, much better now. And what about you? Did you just come out of the Sky Dome?"

The man smiled. "Yes, I did. A bit of a surprise that. I met someone new. And this time, *she* won the lottery." He fingered his locater/partnering band. It was blinking blue this time.

"I'm so happy for you," I said. "You must be the luckiest man around, being able to view the skies so many times. What are the chances of that happening, huh?"

"I know! It's... well, I guess I'm just lucky."

"So, what did you think of the sky this time?"

"Ah, about that. Remember our conversation last year, when you said it didn't look real? I swear, they must have done something about it. I mean, I had no complaints, but it looks so much more real than ever before. I... I don't know how to describe it but it just looks so damn realistic!"

I smiled. I couldn't say anything of course. Couldn't tell him it was me who modeled the new sky, rebuilt the arrays and the screens from scratch. The Secular Authorities had made sure I'd been sworn to secrecy.

"Yes, it *is* realistic, isn't it?" I said.

He gave me a long, hard questioning look. Then he nodded. "Ah, I think I understand." He winked and gave me a smile. "Good on you! Good on you!"

I was about to say something when I saw someone walking across the plaza toward us.

"Well, I've got to go," he said. "I see my wife approaching. Enjoy the fountain play, my friend." He waved a goodbye and I saw him embrace the newfound love of his life. They walked away and I never saw the man again.

HIGHER

ELIZA VITRI HANDAYANI

The window hasn't been opened for days and the curtains haven't been parted. The smell of clove and weed cigarettes dances in the air to the trance music that pumps the room. The thirty men and five women slouch on the floor or on the long sofa dappled with cigarette burns. Some bounce their heads, some chase the swirling light pattern inside the translucent coffee table. The view outside the window shows the dark buildings and blinking pale lights of northern Jakarta.

It's Saturday evening, the last weekend before Ramadan, their last chance to cut loose before they have to restrict themselves for a whole month. Since Friday they have been moving in and out of this karaoke room, the rooftop dance floor, and a huge club next door. Some of them have been here since Wednesday, some went to work at eight and returned after five, some called in sick, some forgot they had jobs.

The two guys dancing on the coffee table know Patar from work, the guy passed out in the bed, in the concealed bedroom behind the bathroom, knows him from some party, Adisti and Risa have known him since high school. Patar is the glue holding all the people in the room together. He walks out of the bathroom, having showered and wearing fresh clothes, and announces that he has to leave the party and take his girlfriend to a movie. Whines and objections spiral up from around the room.

"Tar, you can't leave. This is *your* thing."

"Just tell her you're sick."

Everyone knows better than to suggest that Patar bring Yeni, his girlfriend of six years, to the party. They understand Patar goes to her whenever he wants to be 'good,' and to the people in this room whenever he wants to be 'bad.' Adisti and Risa have slept with Patar on separate occasions – it is much safer to explore your desires with the people you trust – and whenever they meet Yeni at weddings or outings, they chat lightly about fashion or the news.

"How the fuck are you gonna go to her and look sober?" asks Risa. The inside of her lips are bleeding, but she cannot feel it. She's been grinding her teeth since Friday night, and she's been out of chewing gum since this afternoon.

Patar isn't worried. "Listen, I promised to take her out tonight before you all asked me to arrange this party. I've never canceled on her before. I'll take her to the movies, drive her home, and come straight back here. All right?"

Adisti grabs his hand. "You can't leave me here."

"Ferdian's still here," says Patar, pointing to him. "He'll watch out for you."

Adisti isn't really concerned, was just trying to make Patar stay. Three out of the five girls in the room have their boyfriends with them, so only she and Risa are theoretically available to be hit on – but Adisti trusts that no one in the room would dare bother her because she is a close friend of Patar and Ferdian.

With strong jawline, long sideburns, and fierce wide eyes, Patar radiates the charisma needed to be the leader of their group. His next-in-command, Ferdian, is tall, although a bit chubby, with a round and clean-shaven face. Girls like him for his fair skin, unintimidating boyish look, and overall happy-go-lucky attitude about life. Adisti looks comfortable in a loose golden dress, accessorized with a black choker necklace and a rhinestone bracelet. She likes to paint and doesn't like to think too much about her clothes, but she wants to look nice all the time, so she wears dresses everywhere. Risa, on the contrary, looks painfully immaculate in a tight-fitting black tube dress. Her face is made up as if she were going to a wedding, her hair falls in curls around her bare shoulders. She is an intern at a national newspaper, and she always struggles with deadlines. Usually she joins Patar's parties only for a few hours. Adisti is surprised Risa has stayed for two days this time. Earlier, Adisti saw her talking to the club's bathroom attendant, and security guard. She wonders if Risa is working on an assignment.

Adisti closes her eyes, and a shadow of a man drifts to her. Ikhsan. The last time she entered the club next door with him, a host of high-school-aged prostitutes flocked to him. The girls blocked their way before they even made it to the bar and started whispering in his ears. Ikhsan reached out to Adisti and brushed the length of her arm while apologizing to the girls. One of them pushed ahead and approached her.

"Excuse me, Miss, is he your boyfriend?"

"Yes, he is."

"Sorry, we didn't know," the girl said, and led her friends away.

That was November last year. He left her in February. It is now September. Adisti still reaches for the memories of their times together whenever she needs something to make her smile. As she loses herself, he is with her again, and the time long gone becomes now again.

X

Risa first asked to come to one of Patar's parties in their junior year in college. Patar scanned her ankle-length skirt and round glasses and said, "I don't know what you're talking about."

Risa had to chase him. "If you're worried about the little-miss-perfect act, it's just so my parents won't ask questions. You of all people must know the importance of discretion, right?"

After inviting her a few times to his karaoke parties, then alcohol parties, Patar finally invited Risa to drug parties. The first time she visited the clubs in this area she got the idea to do an article on the people that worked there.

She wants to interview the bartender pouring her beer and ask him how he feels about dispensing haram drinks to people, especially now that Ramadan approaches. She wants to ask him if he enjoys his job, if he makes more money than his neighbors who work as couriers at offices or custodians at shopping malls, and if so, does his job earn him more respect in his neighborhood? She wants to ask the locker attendant how he feels every time an older man holding a teenage prostitute asks to get his bag – does he show up at work struggling with his conscience? Does he come home every morning to his wife and kids feeling proud to have fulfilled his obligation to provide for them? Does he tell himself 'these people get earthly pleasures, I get heavenly bliss'? Or is he completely desensitized?

They are a physical part of the world of the rich folk who come here to flush money down the toilet, but do they really feel they are a part of it? If not, how does it feel to be so close to a world without ever belonging to it? Also, when they witness celebrities, or state or military officials, doing scandalous things at the club, what keeps them from telling the tabloids or the police? Or posting their pictures anonymously on the internet? Do they sense that they have the power to ruin the famous, the rich, and the powerful? Or is the sense of powerlessness so deeply ingrained within them?

Risa isn't sure how to get these people to open up to her. So she figures she'll just get high first. So far this is what she has: the attendant of the women's bathroom has been working there for six years, the guy who sweeps the club's floor is being paid Rp 400,000 a month, and the bartender is a Muslim who will be fasting when Ramadan comes.

Patar says something to Ferdian, who nods in reply, then Patar leaves the room.

"And he's gone," Ferdian says, sitting down next to Risa.

"Like you never did that," says Risa.

Ferdian has a girlfriend too: a co-worker from West Java who wears the hijab. He has mentioned her to his parents in West Sumatra, he told them that she was very kind and loving, and that she practiced Islamic values devoutly. Their reaction: "That's nice, son. But we would rather you marry a West Sumatran girl."

He runs his fingers across Risa's palms. "Your hands are sweaty. Are you all right?"

"They're always sweaty. Do you remember the last time we were here?"

Ferdian nods.

X

It was a month earlier. Risa was trying to get away from an acquaintance of Patar, a cop, who had been after her all night. "I just got back from Palembang," he said after he found her on the club's main floor, in front of the DJ who spun his magic on a high silver pedestal. Behind him a one-eyed octopus spurted green and purple tentacles all over the room. "Caught a crook there and brought him back here. Hard work."

"I imagine," said Risa.

"You look so pretty. For a second I thought you were my ex-girlfriend."

"Smooth."

"No, seriously. If you need anything tonight, just let me know, OK? I can take you to any club you want, get us in, and get us free drinks *all night*. I'm the one who got us that space, you know." He pointed to the largest balcony on the second floor where their party gathered.

At that time Risa thought she would rather be waterboarded than go anywhere with this one-man embodiment of everything that disgusted her about Indonesia. She racked her brain for a way to untangle herself from him without offending him. She feared for her safety.

Luckily Ferdian came. "Here's water for you, Ris."

"Are you guys an item?" asked the cop.

Risa quickly nodded.

"Aw, man." The cop tapped Ferdian's shoulder. "Bro, I didn't know. I'll leave you two alone."

Ferdian slipped his arms around Risa's waist and whispered, "You don't mind, do you?"

She turned around and their lips found each other like metal and magnet. Their tongues made love in their mouths. Risa knew she should stop, but it felt so delicious, so right.

"You knew that I had a crush on you all through high school, didn't you? That's why you kept borrowing my notes, you knew I would always lend them to you," said Risa.

"Really? I had no idea."

"I would rewrite my notes so they would be neat and complete, and you returned them with cookie crumbs between the pages."

"Why didn't you tell me sooner? I never thought you would be interested in someone like me."

They kissed again. Ferdian looked at his watch. It was seven in the morning. "I have a meeting with a client at nine. Can I take you home?"

"I'm still high. Can't you cancel?"

"Unfortunately no."

Risa knew Ferdian was not like Patar, who often said, "When I cheat, it's only my body, my heart remains faithful to Yeni." Risa knew Ferdian would just drive her home and then shower, change, and meet his client. She would not even try to seduce him to have sex with her. Yet there was something in his voice that made her want to go with him, away from their group, away from that cop, from that man dancing by himself, his eyes all white as his pupils rolled back so far inside his skull. Perhaps she should call it a night, sleep, and then ask Ferdian to dinner. See if he would leave his girlfriend for her.

She stayed at the club. The next day Ferdian called her. He had never called her out of the blue before. They talked about how she had made sure that Adisti got home safe, about when they would all go partying again. After he hung up, Risa decided:

he called because he wanted to see if there would be problems between them, there was no way he called to ask her out, just the two of them, because last night's kisses had meant something to him. Guys don't make girls like her their real girlfriends. On the phone she had assured him that there would be no problems, they could forget about what happened. Easy. She had done the right thing.

X

"Patar's screwed," Ferdian says. "Yeni is growing more and more suspicious."

"Really?" says Risa.

"Do you know her father's a cop? And her mom teaches Sunday school? I can't even imagine what will happen to Patar – and to us – if she ever finds out and tells mommy and daddy."

X

Around 9 p.m. Ferdian feels his cell-phone vibrate in his pants pocket. He, Risa, and Adisti are dancing on the club's main stage. The green tentacles of the octopus caress their faces.

Ferdian slams his phone to his ear. "What's up, Tar?"

"The movie's over, but Yeni doesn't want to go home. She insists on meeting you guys."

Ferdian presses his phone even closer to his ear. "What did you tell her?"

"I have to cut the night short because I promised to meet some friends. Can't some of you go to that ice cream place that opens late in Senayan? I can pretend that's where I'm meeting you guys. We'll chat for half an hour and then I'll drive her home and you'll go back to the club."

"I don't think we can do that. We can meet her at the café on the club's first floor."

"I am *not* taking her to the club!"

"Then?"

"Go back to the room. See if anyone's willing to meet me at Senayan."

"Goddamn it, Tar!" Ferdian hangs up and pulls Risa's and Adisti's arms. "We've got to go back."

Just like that, Adisti is yanked out of her reverie. She was just making out with Ikhsan on this very dance floor.

Confused and disoriented, she moves along with Ferdian who is leading her and Risa out of the club. Outside, the smoke-ridden air gives way to fresher air with hints of garbage stench. Men approach them offering taxis, little children swarm to them cupping their hands. Among them Adisti notices a plump woman with gray hair spun behind her head and a baby held to her chest by a fading batik scarf. The woman moves toward her and says, "Miss, please give."

Adisti almost laughs. This woman is always here every time Adisti visits this club. Always with a baby in her scarf. The baby doesn't seem to have grown since the last time Adisti was here with Ikhsan. She wonders if before the woman goes out begging she picks a baby who looks sickest and most fragile.

"Miss, have pity."

Adisti shakes her hand loose from Ferdian's and reaches for her purse.

The children cheer behind the woman. "Come here, come here, this one's gonna give."

Adisti remembers the last time she was here with Ikhsan he gave this woman Rp 10,000. She tries to find a Rp 10,000 bill in her wallet, but she only sees Rp 50,000 notes. She feels angry. "Sorry."

"But Miss—"

"Sorry, I'm not Ikhsan! If I were Ikhsan, I'd give it to you."

Adisti runs away from the woman and the children. This club, this street, this city conceals landmines of their memories together. Every time she sees the beggar with the baby, or their favorite pizza restaurant, or the kiosk where they bought their beer, the past would explode and engulf the present.

One evening Ikhsan sat by an orange bus stop near Risa's office waiting for her. She was going to tell him something funny – something she preferred not to say via text message. His face brightened as he caught sight of her walking out of her office building. It was last November, but Adisti still sees him there every evening, drinking from his water bottle, waiting for her to tell him the funny news.

Ikhsan is a humanitarian worker and he doesn't make much. Sometimes when they went out Adisti paid the check. Last time they went here Ikhsan bought her a pill. Later in the night he asked for his money back.

"Are you serious?"

"Yes, please. I'm out of cash. I need to buy some water."

Still, he always gave to beggars who approached him. After he left her, Adisti started giving to beggars too. And when she does he is there with her. She can see his arm reaching out to pass the Rp 10,000 bill. He is there through her. And the world lights up all around her – as it did whenever she was with him – as if the stars suddenly drop from the sky and hover just a meter above their heads.

Adisti stares at her rhinestone bracelet. Once Ikhsan asked her if she didn't like to wear jewelry.

"I like simplicity," she said.

"I bet you look great with a simple necklace and perhaps earrings."

Adisti can't bring herself to wear earrings, but after he left her she bought some necklaces and bracelets, and now she wears them everywhere, as if saying to him: These are the marks you left on me. Here is who I've become since you. Do you think by leaving me you can remove your traces from around me? And within me? Do you really think staying away will erase you from my memory? I may no longer hold your body, but your image I'll hold forever. When you first told me about yourself under the Hanuman statue, high on his arch at Pancoran, you sealed my romantic fate: I knew every man after you would be a stand-in for you, a partial substitute. I will look for pieces of you in them – the humanitarian worker, the one who wears rope necklaces, the one with a saw scar on his left hand, the one with the first-class law degree, the one who came from that small town in the northern part of Java, the one who opens himself up to me with such intensity since the first evening we met, the one with excellent memory and Mentos scent in his breath, who always ends his text messages with 'kisses'… Maybe if I gather each of these pieces, from each of those men, somehow I will recover you. Or I can go on giving to beggars and relive you, relive us. I am your lover, your victim, your curse. I will take your image and paint it on my canvas, on the city's walls, again and again, until I get it right. Maybe then, knowing you will never vanish, I can set you aside. Because if you were to vanish, Ikhsan, if I forget you, like they tell me to, then a slice of myself will vanish with you. And I will no longer be able to explain who I am.

X

"If you don't trust me, why did you say yes when I proposed?" Patar says as he and Yeni walk out of the movie theater in Senayan, South Jakarta. Long purple neon lights illuminate a staircase ahead of them. Upset, Patar dashes down the stairs, but then he realizes they may be too steep for Yeni on high heels, so he climbs back up to help her.

"It's not that I don't trust you, I just want to meet your friends. You see them every other weekend, yet I only ever met Ferdian, Adisti, and Risa."

"I don't think they're gonna show up." They reach the parking lot where two attendants in orange uniform are busy pushing cars to make way for ones that want to get out. "Let's go home."

Yeni jerks her arm free. "No! Show me you have nothing to hide or we're done."

"Are you insane?"

Yeni takes her car keys from Patar's hand and climbs into the driver's seat.

For a moment Patar imagines taking his girlfriend to the room where thirty-five of his friends greet her with their eyes bulging out and teeth clanging. How is he to explain why the party is held at a dodgy karaoke place next to an infamous drug club? What will he say? What should he do?

He walks away from the car and calls Ferdian. "Hey. Is anyone going to meet us at that ice cream place?"

Across the city, in the karaoke room, Ferdian shakes his head. "Sorry, Tar. Not gonna happen."

Patar curses out loud. "Then I have to take her there."

"Are you out of your mind?"

"She insists, all right? What am I supposed to do?"

"Is that Patar?" a guy beside Ferdian shouts. "When is he coming back?"

"If he's coming back, he's gonna bring Yeni," says Ferdian.

"What?" Everyone in the room objects almost in unison. "No!"

"Tar, you know what, you don't have to come back," shouts one.

"Don't sacrifice us for your girlfriend. Her father's a cop, for god's sake," says another.

"Yeah, we're not coming down for her."

In the parking lot Patar is fuming. "Fuck you all. I planned the party for you!"

The guy beside Ferdian grabs the phone and says, "Listen, can't you slip her something? With luck she'll just pass out on the way."

"That's actually a good idea." Patar glances at Yeni in the car. She's giving him the evil eye. "OK, tell everyone we're coming."

He opens the car door on Yeni's side. "Fine, I'll take you to see my friends. But I'm hungry. Can we have something to eat first?"

Yeni hugs him, whispers thanks, and slides to the passenger's seat.

As Patar turns on the engine, he feels a small bag of powder in his pocket.

X

A little past ten o'clock Ferdian receives a message from Patar that they are close. He shouts, "Listen everyone, Patar and Yeni are almost here!"

A loud "Fuuuuuucccckkkkk" thunders through the room.

Some people scurry to the bathroom to wash their faces, a guy runs out to buy more gum, the guys wearing shades decide to flee to the club next door, or to the rooftop dance floor, a girl splashes water on the bathroom's floor to wash away the vomit. Ferdian walks around telling the people dancing on the coffee table to sit down, and taps the shoulders of the couple making out too passionately. Risa collects the empty water bottles off the floor. Adisti sprays air freshener around the room, turns on the television, and switches the machine's mode from trance to karaoke.

Several minutes later there is a knock on the door.

Everyone sits tensely, looking at the door. Adisti, Risa, and a few others stand before the door like football players anticipating a free kick.

"Ready?" says Ferdian. He signals to everyone and opens the door.

They see Patar and Yeni by the doorframe. Everyone stops breathing.

Risa and Adisti stretch out their arms. "Yeeennniii, nice to see you!"

Yeni falls into Adisti's embrace. "Nice to see you too." She hugs Risa next. "It's been so long."

Behind her, Risa exchanges relieved glances with Adisti. Yeni seems more trashed than either of them.

Adisti leads Yeni to the sofa. She asks if she wants to sing, if she is tired. Yeni puts her head on Adisti's shoulder. Adisti signals to the guy near the switch to dim the lights. Sometimes she feels sorry for Yeni. Sometimes she thinks Yeni refuses to see signs of Patar's secret activities. Adisti feels an urge to slap her cheeks and shout, 'Wake up. Look around you. Girls like you are bound to be fooled. You need to see the world. The man you think loves you can just drug you or leave you for no reason. You can wake up one morning and find that he is not who you thought he was, that everything is not what you thought it was. Why should I feel sorry for you when there are mothers with babies begging outside this building?'

Ten minutes later Yeni passes out on the sofa.

X

Eleven o'clock. A guy is singing a house version of a popular song, several others are dancing around him. On the sofa Adisti stares into her cell phone. A message from Ikhsan: `Hi, Dis. Holy fasting month is coming. Let it be a fresh start for both of us. Please forgive me for all the pain I might have caused you.`

Adisti thinks: If I ever was going to forgive him, the time is now, Allah will not forgive those who cannot forgive his fellow men. She types: `I forgive you. Please forgive me too.`

On the other end of the sofa, Risa mutters to Ferdian, "Fuck my project. I tried talking to the guy who sweeps the club's floor. I totally expected him to be nice to me, but he was very rude. 'Why you wanna know?' he barked."

"Why should he be nice to you?"

"Eh, I noticed he existed, unlike everyone else?"

"But you flush one million easy to mess your brain for one night, and he has to clean your vomit for a whole month and not make as much."

"You're right. Are you not seeing your girlfriend this weekend?"

"She's in Bandung with her parents." Then: "Talk to the cleaning ladies before you leave. Didn't you say they like to eat breakfast in the supply closet in the women's bathroom?"

"Yeah. Around seven usually. Girls are puking their guts out in the sinks and those women just sit there eating coconut rice."

"Tell them you're hungry, but don't want to order food from the club because it's too expensive. Ask them to buy you coconut rice, give them a large bill, but not too large, tell them to keep the change. Once you have your rice, you'll have to hide with them in the supply closet, and then you can talk to them."

"That's a great idea, Ferdi. Thanks."

"Sure." He rests his head on her shoulder. Once, after they kissed a month earlier, Ferdian wondered what it would be like to date Risa. But he could imagine what Risa would say if he asked her out. He knew she knew what she had to do.

Out there, there are obligations to meet, family expectations to fulfill. Out there we live in the hours, rowing our boat on a river of cause and effect that flows mercilessly onward, but in rooms like this we can do what we like with the hours, spray the past into the present, encase the present in a bubble, shove the future out the window and draw the curtains. In rooms like this Ferdian and Risa can hold each other's hands.

X

Patar comes out of the bathroom and sits on the sofa next to Yeni. His face is wet. He kisses her hair. Patar doesn't smoke, so when the smell of nicotine or clove suffocates him, he likes to seek refuge in Yeni's hair. It smells like a field of strawberries. He whispers, "Baby, we have to go home. It's almost midnight. Your parents will be worried."

Yeni circles her arms around his shoulders without opening her eyes.

"It's OK. Just sleep. I'll wake you up when we're close." He slowly lifts her up in his arms like a bride. "Say bye to Adisti, Ferdian, and Risa."

Still with her eyes closed Yeni waves her hand. Adisti, Risa, and Ferdian get up and wave back.

The room holds its breath as Patar heads for the door. When it finally closes behind him, the room reanimates. People shout out their joy. They resume dancing, necking, lighting up cigarettes. Adisti, Risa, and Ferdian can finally exhale.

"Well done," Ferdian says.

"Up?" says Risa.

They cheer with excitement. Ferdian reaches into his pocket and presents three white pills on his palm. Each swallows one and grabs a bottle of water. Holding each other's hands, the three walk out of the room and take the stairs to the rooftop. They can see flashes of blue from up ahead, the music booms louder and louder, they answer its call faster and faster, with each step up and up, higher and higher.

FOR YOUR MERRY DAYS ARE OVER

MICHAEL AARON GOMEZ

Two men stayed alive, crouched in the vault's corners, with guns in their hands and prayers on their lips. They were the remaining members of the Kruxial Boize six-man armed robbery group. One was called Jhunel, the other Dodong. This was their first caper. And now it was looking to be their last – expecting the same end as the others, lying there shredded by the full-auto submachine gun fire from the police sent to raid them. Other casualties from the firefight were a couple of bank clerks, customers, and the manager. Any moment now the black-clad SWAT team could burst into the vault and pump them full of holes. No use for all this money now. They had only .38 paltiks against the cops' H&K MP5s.

It happened so fast and off-script. Four of them were to pose as customers and sit far enough apart from each other to cover more ground. Jhunel and Dodong were to barge in, disarm the guards, and keep everybody else's heads down. They were to shoot a guard in the leg to hurry things along. Once everybody had been tied up, the rest of the gang would rise up and keep watch – firing warning shots – while Jhunel and Dodong dragged the bank manager by the neck toward the bank vault. An accomplice from Tinago was to wait outside the nearby McDonalds' in their getaway van, itself stolen. The whole operation was to last for just five minutes. Classic get-in-get-out.

The gang had planned this for a month, even rehearsed it. They had scoped out and memorized the interior of the BPI Perdices branch. Tripped alarms posed no problem either, for they had bet they'd be able to escape before the cops came. Tagalog action movies had taught them that the police are always late for everything.

But Michael accidentally dropped his gun on the floor before Jhunel and Dodong even got out of the van, inciting chaos and screaming, which provoked Junmar and Edwin and Jhon Mark to shoot the two guards dead, forcing the other two gangsters to hurry into the bank alarm bells ringing in their skulls, all six of them working on the fly like headless chickens, looking for the bank manager. Everything was fucked.

By Jhunel's estimate they'd been in there for ten minutes too long. Even if the cops were always late, he hadn't counted on them being *that* late. And still no sign of the bank manager. If they had just learned how to make bombs they'd have had no need of him. But there was nobody to teach them – there were no Muslim terrorist cells in Dumaguete City. Fifteen, twenty, twenty-five minutes had gone by before they found the guy. He'd been cowering in the stall in the toilet, his feet up on the throne. Jhunel held him at gunpoint to lead them to the bank vault. Just when the manager had opened the vault doors they heard sirens, megaphone-yells and crunching boots, and Michael felt something warm streaming down his leg.

Jhunel put a bullet in the manager's head and they rushed to shovel as much cash as they could into their flour sacks. Up on the toilet's ceiling was a vent they could use to escape, but no one knew where it led, plus the crawl space seemed too small for a person – even those as spectral as the Kruxial Boize – too small and too narrow for a person carrying sacks of cash. The only windows were in the bank manager's office, but they opened out to the streets now filled with cops. A SWAT van was parked on the sidewalk. Now the six men's legs were soaked. No choice. They had to fight their way out, and take hostages. Michael led the way. He used a yelling old woman as a human shield. He made his demands with warning shots, which the police answered with a hail of hot lead. He fell and stopped his demands.

When Junmar, Edwin, and Jhon Mark blew their shields' heads off and decided to meet their fates on the bank steps, like brave cowboys, Jhunel and Dodong knew it was all over. They lugged two sacks of cash each and fled to the vault. None of them had imagined making their last stand on their first operation. The plan was foolproof - they just had shitty execution and wasted too much time. They had no contingency plans for accidents – Dodong wanted to blame Michael for dropping the fucking gun, but Jhunel shushed him. "It wasn't his fault. We just panicked out there."

Dodong burst into tears while Jhunel fought back his. They had seen their four friends ripped apart by unfeeling SMGs.

The SWAT team searched the bank for them, releasing the bank customers.

Jhunel imagined the SWAT team's arsenal – he had seen enough police movies to have his own set of stock images – and considered their chances. He could see their shining M-16s, thick body armor, grenades, and a battering ram, the small kind. He wondered if the battering ram could actually smash through the vault's reinforced steel door. Maybe they'd use grenades or maybe they had like, tiny bombs for times like this.

"We should have borrowed one," Jhunel snickered.

Dodong looked at him funny and asked what was up. Jhunel said it was nothing. "I'm just scared."

"Me too," said Dodong.

They checked their ammo. Jhunel wondered if he could aim for the policemen's heads when they finally blew that door open. He probably could, but he'd most likely be dead before he could even lift his .38. It felt like hell inside the vault. There were no windows, only steel. The two remaining Kruxial Boize fanned themselves with the bills from their sacks. Jhunel and Dodong had never felt more tired in their lives, even more than after their most strenuous, full-blooded rehearsals.

Dance rehearsals, that is.

X

The Kruxial Boize had been a dance group.

It was Jhunel who'd assembled them three years earlier, when the TV variety show *Showtime* had called for dance groups nationwide to battle it out over a period of months, for the grand prize of three million pesos. He called his mates Dodong and Michael from the barangay, Edwin from college, and Junmar and Jhon Mark from high school.

They had been rejected from the city's other, bigger dance groups, also vying for a spot on Manila's *Showtime*. 'Not really what we're looking for,' the refrain went. The six men had all been amateur dancers in some capacity. All of them had performed in school programs, barangay contests, city fiestas, intermission numbers in minor beauty pageants, backup dancing in talent shows, and political rallies. People liked them well enough – save for Dumaguete's star dancers. Jhunel once hit one of them in the face, a gay dancer named Dondie, the go-to trainer of high schools preparing for Founder's Day events, notorious for his pink fan and his foul temper, which Jhunel tasted for the whole night of practice for a minor contest at university.

"You don't know how to dance, you stupid," the homo would insult him. "Why don't you just go home and stop wasting my time, why do you even call yourself a dancer?"

Jhunel said it was the fan that made him snap. "I can dance," he told Dondie. "Fucking faggot, I know how to."

Post-practice, Dondie had made him stay behind for more humiliation. The homo kept hitting Jhunel with the fan and yelling at him until he stood up and knocked Dondie on his ass with a hook to the jaw. He pummeled the trainer, who in short order began yelping for help. *Like a scalded dog*, he thought as he gave Dondie the beatdown of his life. Soon the police came and arrested Jhunel. They had him apologize to Dondie at the station, where he kept screaming for Jhunel to be thrown in jail. The cops just snickered at him. Jhunel said sorry, smiling at Dondie's grape-colored face.

It turned out that the world of dancers was smaller than he thought: Dondie tattled to the other star dancers (most of them gay) and they blacklisted Jhunel, plus everybody else who might be related to him, however distantly. They were to be treated like lepers. Dodong and the rest knew what Jhunel had done, why they'd been rejected, but they remained loyal to their friend.

"That's what you get," they said. "Fuck you. We'll win the grand prize on our own, we'll show all you fucking homos, suck our dicks."

Thus, did the Kruxial Boize come into being.

Jhunel had thought up the name: he didn't know what it meant, he just liked how it looked on paper, and how it sounded. Their only problem was that they were strapped for cash. They couldn't afford the trip to Cebu for the *Showtime* auditions, scheduled three months hence. Don't even think about costumes. Not one of them was employed, half were students. Dodong, Michael and Jhunel relied on intermittent rackets – beauty pageants and talent shows for money. The other three couldn't rely on extra cash, since their parents didn't think much of dancing and would have refused them outright had they revealed the Kruxial Boize and their plans.

Infuriating them further were Dondie and the rest rubbing their faces in it: Dondie's group, named Primal Objectz, was already preparing for their Cebu trip, posting photos of their costumes (silvery shining ensembles) on Facebook and Instagram, with captions reading, 'Showtime hir we cum!!!!'. Jhunel wanted to wring the homo's neck, show him which of them *really* couldn't dance. Didn't even know how to name a group properly. The rest of the group grew angry, then despondent, and then dispirited. Their self-appointed leader had to do something.

Good thing he lived in Tinago.

He had contacts with people in the "hood" – at least those with toes dipped in the underworld, anyway – and he asked for connections, an "in" to the city's shabu trade, whose routes originated from Cebu and snaked through the rest of Central Visayas. Asked what the hell he needed the money for, Jhunel said it was for his sick grandmother. His drug-dealing friends laughed at him. He admitted everything. They laughed at him some more but introduced him to their supplier – an obese Chinaman who had gold teeth, and who also laughed at him, but agreed to supply him with a half-kilo of shabu every two weeks, their cuts 60/40.

And so Jhunel began his life as a businessman. He sold drugs to government workers, to office employees, to rich college kids, and soon his business pleased the Chinaman enough to raise his product to a kilo per week. Their cuts became 70/30, but it still left Jhunel with enough breathing room. He had enough sense not to flaunt his money. It didn't take long before Jhunel earned enough to have costumes sewn. Again he oversaw the design: a complete outfit, comprising red sleeveless shirts studded with shiny pinheads and glittering black pants – yellow thunderbolts streaked across the shirtfronts and along the pants' legs. He spent three nights drawing up the designs.

The Kruxial Boize wore these costumes during the robbery.

Jhunel didn't flaunt his money, but he wasn't greedy either. He gave extra cash to the other members, bought shoes and other things they needed, and each time they met there was always top-notch food and mid-shelf drinks. When Dodong asked him about his sudden wealth Jhunel just smiled and squeezed Dodong's shoulder and said he found himself a job. Dodong knew better than to ask more questions, but it was fishy: Jhunel had stopped smoking Fortune Reds/Mighty Reds and switched to Marlboros and Lucky Strikes. And the kicker was, he bought them in packs.

X

In the vault Dodong asked if Jhunel really sold shabu. Through the steel walls they could hear faint human noises. The leader was staring at his gun, and he looked at his friend and said he won the Suertres lotto game ten times. That is why he got so rich. And then he laughed. Dodong kept looking at him funny. He told Jhunel there was nothing wrong with selling drugs. Really nothing. They made it to Cebu, didn't they? What else could you have done?

Jhunel said maybe this was all payback from God.

He certainly didn't believe in one during his drug-dealing days. God never gave him money, no matter how many times he prayed. So then he had no problem letting Junmar and Jhon Mark in on his business. When they'd asked him where he was getting his money, he'd told them straight up he was a drug pusher – he'd hoped he'd sounded too incredible for them.

But they didn't laugh at him. The duo wanted in, too. They'd never seen so much cash in their lives. And plus, they were too embarrassed to ask Jhunel for more money. After all he was still their leader, so they figured they might as well start hustling too. They could buy clothes every week, and brand new cell phones. They could finally play DOTA as long as they wanted. The Chinaman scoffed at Jhunel when he asked him to up his supply of shabu to two kilos a week.

"One and a half," the Chinaman said.

Jhunel accepted and the three of them divvied up the product, each of them receiving equal cuts from the sales. That was how much Jhunel loved his Kruxial Boize.

His only instruction was: "Never get high on your own supply."

Which they promptly did. They started skipping meetings and practices, and when they did show up they were clearly in no shape to even dance a two-step. The other Kruxial Boize wanted them out, Jhunel did too, but he was scared they might not make it to Cebu, much less *Showtime*, if they were incomplete. It was some kind of superstition to him. But he had no choice – the three million pesos was more important. He regretted letting Junmar and Jhon Mark in on the racket, but he thought them weaklings for succumbing to the drug, too gutless to keep the millions in view. Jhunel and the rest gave the two offenders beatdowns and then sent them on their way. They hadn't even received their costumes.

There was silence for half a year until they returned from Cebu, and found Junmar and Jhon Mark asleep on the streets, all strung-out and ghostly, their addictions having finally devoured them. Their parents had disowned them, kicked them out of their houses. Now they lived under the yellow lampposts of the Boulevard, begging everything that moved for cash and scraps. The two still wore the same shirts they'd worn the last time the Kruxial Boize had met complete.

Jhunel took pity on them and let them shack up with him at Tinago. He took care of them while they detoxed, saw demons, and formicated. He fed them and supported them until they were as close as possible to normal. During recovery he apologized to them for fucking them up.

"You won't see drugs here," he told them. "I'm not a pusher anymore."

It was during this time that Jhunel toyed with the idea of reforming the Kruxial Boize – this time as a criminal group. Sort of like gangsters, he thought. First he thought about becoming carnappers, but realized he didn't know what to do with the cars they'd steal. And then he thought about becoming burglars, but he figured preparations would waste too much time. He'd had enough of waste. Just thinking about it made him want to hurt someone. Dondie's mocking face popped up in his dreams and he imagined ramming a boiling hot steel rod up his ass. Finally he decided they would become bank robbers.

X

The noises outside the vault grew louder. Jhunel and Dodong gripped their guns, holding their cash-sacks against their chests, sweating blood and piss. Combat boots thudded on the floor and in their heads. The last members of the Kruxial Boize waited for the inevitable. They both knew they were going to hell, and they didn't want to go there alone. But the noises peaked and then passed. The two men didn't know whether to be relieved. *Just get this whole thing over with.* Jhunel checked and rechecked his ammo, spinning the .38's cylinder so fast it looked ready to fly off. Dodong wiped his sweat on his shirtfront. The room stank of piss.

They prayed.

X

Michael was the first to join this latest venture. Next was Edwin. Dodong was the hardest to convince. He didn't plan to be a criminal. He said, "I'd rather be poor than a criminal. Don't include me. Go look for someone else."

But Jhunel was stubborn, he could only do something if the Kruxial Boize were there, complete. He had staked too much on the group to turn his back on them, and he'd fucked up human lives in the process. He still didn't believe in God, but at least he wanted to do right by his friends.

The Kruxial Boize had failed. They reached the second round of auditions at Cebu but they were beaten by Primal Objectz. Dondie gave Jhunel a withering mocking smirk. Furious, Jhunel stomped toward the homo, wanting to rip his head off his neck, only to be restrained by the rest of the Boize. The judges would have none of his antics and promptly blacklisted them from *Showtime*, in perpetuity.

"No matter how you shuffle your members," they said, "no matter how often you change your names, you won't be allowed to join any more *Showtime* contests."

The guards dragged them out of the audition area. Dondie gave Jhunel and his crew another smirk – and even blew them a kiss as they were leaving. Their only response was to yell "Faggot!" which now had no effect.

Even if they'd beaten up Dondie and his group, they still wouldn't have won.

Jhunel only realized this when he and Dodong were hiding in the bank vault. There was nothing he could have done. The judges voted them in, not us. *Maybe they'd known about us, about what I did to that faggot Dondie.* But complaining wouldn't have done them any good. They'd just have labeled the Kruxial Boize childish and sore losers. And he shouldn't have threatened Dondie's life. He laughed at this now, inside the vault, and then he felt sorry for Dodong who ended up in there with him – he would have preferred to be alone, he was the one who started everything, he was the one who failed his friends, so by rights he should face up to his sins alone. But he wasn't, Dodong was here, Jhunel's most benign friend. He didn't even want a gun until last night. Too afraid of actually using the thing – he'd much rather use it on himself than aim it at something. Yet Jhunel had seen anger slowly consume his friend.

But laughter was the only thing left. He could only laugh at himself, at the fate of the Kruxial Boize, at Dondie and his group. He laughed remembering how he kicked that faggot's ass. His face at the police station was priceless. The color of mangosteen, it had bumps and bruises, bleeding at the mouth's edges, the blood trickling down his chin. He'd relish that image for the rest of his life. And then Jhunel laughed at the success of Primal Objectz, who'd gone on to appear on *Showtime* and then reached the last monthly finals, where they were beaten by the XS Boyz, a group from somewhere in Mindanao Jhunel couldn't remember. The XS Boyz won the whole damn thing, too.

It was Dodong who helped Jhunel secure their equipment. They bought their .38s from a fat retired policeman the Chinaman also supplied. The Chinaman asked them if they were moving into another line of work, and Jhunel answered him yes. At this the fat man smiled at them and bade them good luck. "You going to need it," he said.

The very next day another kilo of shabu arrived for Jhunel.

Jhunel saw that Dodong wanted get-back from their failure at *Showtime* in some form or other. Dodong ached for it, couldn't sleep at night because of it, but he didn't know whether he could really go against his nature and become a cold-blooded criminal. Michael seemed gung-ho. Edwin, too. Junmar and Jhon Mark were too muddled now to do anything else. But Dodong still seemed an iffy addition. And so Jhunel decided to test him.

There was a regular customer who'd been neglecting to pay Jhunel for the past month. He was a college kid, Sillimanian, rich, but you could tell he had been found out and so was being frozen out by the folks, in the hopes that he'd wean himself off the shit. Evidently he hadn't, and the only things he'd paid Jhunel with were addled promises and IOUs. The leader of the Kruxial Boize went to his dealer friends for advice and was told to either get paid or get one less customer. "Don't feed addicts, man," they said. "They bleed you dry only. They don't have cash, cut them loose."

When the kid called him one night, Jhunel had decided.

He called Dodong and asked him to meet. The deal was at a vacant lot somewhere in Banilad, near the city limits of Bacong. It was a weird deal, Jhunel knew, and if the kid was still in his right mind he'd realize things were fishy – transactions were normally conducted at another dealer's safehouse in Tinago. (Police raids were concentrated on Looc, where marijuana was the product of choice.) Dodong got to the spot and saw Jhunel sitting smoking on his motorcycle. He asked him what was up. Jhunel asked him if he was packing. Dodong said he was. "You told me to bring heat."

"Good," Jhunel said.

No more questions.

Soon the kid arrived, all fidgety and shaking. He kept wringing his hands and sniffling. Jhunel wasn't sure whether he was thinking something was fishy or the shabu had melted his mind. But at least he was alone. He didn't ask about Dodong. He only wanted his kicks. Good, Jhunel thought. This scene was something he'd seen often in the movies, so he followed script. He asked for the kid's money first. The kid hedged, hedged, and then hedged some more just to get out of paying. Jhunel feigned anger. He cursed at the kid and told him he hadn't paid him for a month, and he was hurting business.

"I have other customers," Jhunel told the kid, "I'd rather sell only to them."

The kid fell to his knees and cried. He crawled to Jhunel's feet and hugged his knees, begging for just one more hit, "Just one more, one more and I won't buy from you anymore, I'll pay you back for everything!"

Jhunel was stone-faced. Dodong stared at them. He must have been remembering what happened to Junmar and Jhon Mark. His hands were shaking, creeping toward the piece tucked in his waistband. Meanwhile the kid kept groveling.

Minutes of this went by before Dodong got fed up. He yelled "Enough!" marched toward the kneeling kid and put a bullet in his dome. Jhunel had planned to give the instruction himself, but what the fuck, his mouth was flapping in the night breeze as he looked at Dodong, now transformed into a killer. Both men were breathless.

×

Jhunel sensed it was time. He dropped his sacks. They had spent too long in the vault for the SWAT team not to have figured out where they were. He told Dodong to stand up, drop the sacks, and get ready. They were coming. The last members of Kruxial Boize felt their knees shaking, their hands sweating cold. They had pissed every drop inside them. Whatever anger was in their hearts was replaced by surging fear.

The leader of the Kruxial Boize asked Dodong if he had any regrets.

He said he didn't.

Dodong bounced the question back to Jhunel.

"No," he said.

And it was time.

×

The SWAT team reached the vault. They called for the two men to open the door. Surrender peacefully and they wouldn't come to harm.

"Don't be stupid and follow your friends," a voice yelled. "You don't want to die yet, do you?"

The Kruxial Boize didn't answer. Millions of thoughts sprayed across their minds. They couldn't have answered even if they wanted to. The SWAT team began sweet-talking them. Promises were made, offering them safe passage wherever they wanted to go, with a getaway vehicle of their choice. They'd even let them keep their money. Jhunel had seen this scene many times before. This only happened when everything was going to shit. He snickered. He'd thought everything had gone to shit hours earlier. Maybe it was even earlier than that.

Dodong looked at him.

He said nothing.

More yelling from the SWAT leader now: he ordered the two robbers to surrender immediately if they didn't want to get hurt. His harsh tone was back. He hollered that they were preparing a C4 charge to blast through the vault doors, "So this is your last chance. You will die if this explodes. There will be absolutely nothing left of you. Your parents will bury nothing but dust. Do you have wives? Girlfriends? Kids? Do you want them to see you get blown to bits?"

Both Jhunel and Dodong said nothing.

They raised their guns and aimed them at the door.

"Fuck you then!" the SWAT leader shouted. All Jhunel and Dodong could hear was a shattering boom, all they could see was a flash – as bright as the light on the other side. They got blown to the vault's walls, dropping their guns, tasting blood in their mouths and feeling a swelling in their heads. The SWAT team stormed the vault with their SMGs raised and ready to kill. His movie-worthy last stand foiled, Jhunel lay down and closed his eyes. He hurt too much to move. He couldn't even see Dodong. Only his distant moans could be heard. The cops slowly approached. Jhunel could hear someone radioing for an ambulance. He couldn't hear Dodong's groans anymore. He feared the worst.

But then gunshots woke him.

He saw Dodong on his feet, his gun exploding in his hands, and then saw the surprised SWAT team tear him apart with a blizzard of gunfire. Dodong fell and was no more, though he had taken a couple with him. Testosterone and fury pulled Jhunel to his feet and he yelled at the world and let his .38 roar, hitting air, his outburst answered by a crisp brisk volley of SMG fire. He felt every single bullet piercing through his costume, ripping into his flesh, bursting his organs, and then exiting through his back. The pain was unbearable but relieving – he fell, but not alone.

BLEEDING TRASH

TILON SAGULU

“How to get married if I don’t have money? No money bah… really, I’m not kidding,” Dandey smirked, answering the little beggar’s question.

But he did have money, though only enough to get things he wanted like cigarettes and Orange flavored F&N soda – his favorite. Dandey had just finished high school and was still living with his Chinese stepparents, Mr. and Mrs. Kwan. He was officially adopted when he was seven years old, and started living and working at the Kwans’ restaurant, Lady Kwan’s Bak Kut Teh.

After finishing high school Dandey was expected to help his stepparents with the restaurant, especially when a tumor was found in his stepfather’s brain, but what he really wanted was to go to college. He aspired to be a scientist, working in a lab, playing with poisonous chemicals and creating new drugs to treat maladies. All of his school friends were pursuing higher education, but he couldn’t. Sometimes he thought of running away to pursue his ambition, to be selfish at least once in his lifetime, like the way his biological mother (a single parent) ditched him at the Gaya Street Tamu – morning market – when he was only five.

It was still fresh in his memory, as though it happened only yesterday. Whenever he thought about that perplexing moment he would come to the pier and sit on the metal bench where he'd sat for hours waiting for his mother to find him, but she never came. He never stopped asking why she'd left him at the tamu that day, her five-year-old boy who knew nothing about the city. He could've become a beggar just like these kids, he thought, if Mrs. Kwan hadn't taken him home that night.

"Liar!" yelled Sadiah, the thirteen-year-old girl who'd begged money from him, and then laughed. "I bet you have many children now," she added. Her front teeth were rotting, spotted with plaque. Her long black hair was disheveled, but beautifully tinted by the sunset's rays. Dandey was in deep reverie, smoking his last cigarette, watching the sun sinking on the horizon, thinking about his life, and dreaming of collecting the golden ripples on the ocean when the three little beggars approached him with their empty shopping trolley. Amisah, a twelve-year-old girl with a long ponytail, pushed the trolley along the pier, while Sadiah and her ten-year-old brother Udin rode inside. They were begging money from tourists. They told Dandey that they had been begging since morning, but he didn't believe them. Instead of giving them money, Dandey handed them a bag of rambutan he'd bought from one of the lads who wandered about the pier selling fruit. After a moment he handed Sadiah a ten ringgit note.

"You know, a man your age should have a wife and kids by now," Amisah said, while chewing the rambutan flesh. She wiped the juice dribbling from her lips with her t-shirt. There were black and brown stains on her clothes. Dandey wondered if it was the only t-shirt Amisah owned.

"No," Dandey said, his eyes scrutinizing Amisah's dirty face, greasy hair, and her oversized stained t-shirt. "That's not true."

"Yes! It's true."

"Why do you say so?"

"Because I've seen many young couples with kids nowadays," Amisah answered. She sat next to Dandey on the metal bench. He was surprised that she didn't smell as bad as he'd expected. Sadiah got off the shopping trolley and joined Amisah, sitting so close to Dandey that their thighs touched. Her leg felt warm, but he was a little disgusted thinking of her dirt on his skin. Instead of changing his position, Dandey sat still, afraid of offending her. When Sadiah caught Dandey glancing at a rip on the armpit of her shirt, she quickly hid it with her hand. Dandey blushed, and guilt slowly burned his chest.

"I guess I'm not like those young people," Dandey said, looking at the golden horizon, pretending he didn't see the tear in Sadiah's shirt. "I don't want to get married, not because I don't have money, but I just … I don't want to, you know." Dandey paused, thinking about his parents. "It's not easy to raise a family," he added as an afterthought, "I don't have enough money to raise a family anyway."

The orange sky brought him back to the day his mother abandoned him. The same hopelessness and fear he'd felt back then spurted in his stomach. He recalled wandering along Gaya Street alone, terrified and bewildered, and then finally ending up sitting on the metal bench, crying. A few minutes after sunset, a Chinese woman came up to him asking why he was crying and where his parents were – it was Mrs. Kwan. That night Mrs. Kwan had brought him to her shop-house, just above her restaurant, where he met Mr. Kwan, a grumpy man, who'd later become a tenderhearted stepfather. It had been years already, but the feeling of being lost, terrified and confused still gnawed his guts every time he sat on the metal bench, watching the twilight as darkness slowly draped the ocean.

"Bang...give me five ringgit bah," begged Amisah, "five ringgit only." Her voice shattered Dandey's reminiscences. The ten ringgit note he'd given to Sadiah was the last cash he had. Before he handed it to Sadiah he had asked her where her parents were. She told him that her mother was at the fish market, begging for money just like them, and that her father had died when she was young. Her mother didn't have a birth certificate, or an identification card, so she couldn't get a real job. They were illegal denizens of Malaysia – human beings that the legal citizens of Sabah called Pilak. They were ostracized, ignored, and discriminated against like the plastic, paper cups, soda cans, and bottles thrown into the sea; abandoned and drifting aimlessly with the current, belonging to no land, unwelcomed and unwanted.

Why can't they get citizenship? Dandey wondered. *They were born in this land, so technically they're Malaysians, there's no point in sending them back to their grandparents' country because that's not where they belong. But then, where do they truly belong when this land does not welcome them either?*

They sat in silence for a while. Amisah was enjoying her rambutan alone, Sadiah's brother Udin was talking to himself, climbing in and out of the shopping trolley, while Sadiah was in deep reverie, thinking as deeply as Dandey. Her soul was older than her body, and one could easily feel it just by looking into her wistful eyes.

"I didn't choose to beg for money, you know, but it's the only thing I know how to do," Sadiah said. "Of course I'm ashamed of it, but … if you want to dispose of trash, at least put it in the trash can so that it can go where it's supposed to go. Don't simply throw it on the sidewalk, because someone has to clean it up for you later."

"What?" Dandey frowned, looking at Sadiah, confused. *Is she calling herself trash?*

"I'm talking to Amisah," she said. Dandey noticed the rambutan peels all over the sidewalk.

"Who cares?" Amisah said, rolling her eyes. "Nobody cares!"

These little beggars might be lying to me about everything, thought Dandey, but how could he tell? The way they looked – young, dirty, hungry and lost – resonated with him in a subtle way, but he couldn't figure out how or why. There was a sense of brokenness – a universal brokenness – a common language their souls shared. And at the very least, they were humans having human experiences on Earth.

"Abang bah…" Amisah started her cry again, "it's not fair bah you gave her ten ringgit. I only ask for five ringgit…Bang bah…"

"Eh! I gave you a bag of rambutan already and that cost me five ringgit, you know?" Dandey chuckled. "There goes your five ringgit."

"Bang bah…five ringgit only."

"I don't have any more cash, be grateful," Dandey said, "and clean up your mess. Look at all the kulit rambutan. The trash can is just next to you, you know."

"No!" Amisah rolled her tongue. "Once trash always trash, and I'm not going to clean it up … let them rot here. And who cares anyway?"

"Do you have a girlfriend?" Sadiah asked abruptly before Dandey could respond to Amisah's statement.

"What?" He turned to Sadiah. "No! I don't. If I don't want to get married why would I want to have a girlfriend?" He felt a little uncomfortable and he didn't want to mislead Sadiah. *I was not flirty at all, was I?* he thought, *and she's a thirteen-year-old girl!*

"Good," Sadiah said. The wistful quality in her eyes bothered Dandey. It shouldn't be there; it shouldn't exist in any thirteen-year-old.

"If you have a young wife," Sadiah added, "but you don't have money to support a family, your wife is going to turn into a prostitute."

"What? No!"

"It's true!" Amisah added, spitting a rambutan seed out of her mouth. "I've seen it happen to our friend!" They started to speak in a language Dandey couldn't understand. He had never heard it before, but it sounded familiar. When he asked them what they were talking about they said nothing.

"Amisah! Amisah!" Udin yelled. He was still in the trolley, talking to himself and playing some sort of game. "Give me a rambutan!" he said. Amisah threw one to him and he caught it.

"See I've given him one rambutan, I'm sharing this with him. Now, give me my five ringgit!" Amisah said to Dandey.

"No, I don't have any more money."

"But your wallet is so thick!"

"It's *thick*, but empty. I'm telling you the truth," Dandey said. "So do you guys go to school?" They laughed.

"I can't read," Sadiah chuckled, "But she goes to school!" She pointed at Amisah.

"I go to school every Monday and Wednesday, only twice a week," Amisah said. Her eyes sparkled as if she'd just received her five ringgit note. "My teachers are Miss Ain, Mr. Faizul, and Mrs. Tan."

"So you know how to read lah, right?" Dandey asked.

"Almost. I'm still learning," Amisah said, "I can read a li…ttle bit only."

"Why don't you go to school with her?" Dandey asked Sadiah. She smiled, and Dandey couldn't help but stare at her rotting teeth.

"She's scared of being rotan by the teacher!" Amisah laughed, "She said it's painful."

"I don't like being rotan that's why I don't like school," Sadiah added.

"But you have to know at least how to read to survive in this world. Do you guys know there's a public library over there?" Dandey pointed at the Suria Sabah Mall. "You guys can go there for free and read books…" For a second, he forgot that they couldn't read, and then he added, "Maybe they have a learning-how-to-read program, you guys should go there sometimes."

"I don't even have slippers!" Sadiah laughed, "and you want me to go there? People would look at us like filthy trash!"

Dandey glanced at her grimy feet. "Look at their eyes," she said.

"Whose eyes?"

"Everybody's," she said. Dandey hadn't noticed that almost every passerby stared at them, as though it was a crime for them to sit side by side on the metal bench. Some giggled and some knotted their foreheads, as if they'd smelled something nasty, and some simply passed by as if Dandey and the children did not exist at all. *This feels familiar*, Dandey thought and then took a deep breath.

"Where's your mother?" Dandey asked.

"Astaga…How many times do you have to ask?" Sadiah said, "She's at the fish market bah…begging like us."

"Is there a house at the fish market? Where do you guys sleep at night?"

"Well, she has a house," Sadiah said, pointing at Amisah, who was peeling another rambutan with her teeth. "Her house is on water."

"So you live somewhere over there lah, right?" Dandey pointed to the island where a fishing village could be seen. Yellow lights flickered in the village as the sun dimmed, and the purple sky was darker now. Dandey had always wondered what it felt like to live in one of those houses on water.

"No, not there. Just over there," Amisah pointed west. Dandey nodded, pretending he knew exactly where the place was.

"Do you still have your parents, Amisah?" Dandey asked.

"Ya, she does!" Sadiah answered.

"But you only have your mother, right?" Dandey said to Sadiah and she nodded.

"I only have my mother, my brother and my grandmother." She paused. "Grandmother is old." She spaced out.

Dandey couldn't decide whether Sadiah was sad, or merely thinking of something else. Perhaps she was reminiscing again. Amisah threw a rambutan to Udin. He caught it and ate it. They were arguing about something in their language, but the noise didn't bother Sadiah.

"How old were you when you lost your father?" Dandey asked; his voice trembled and his stomach clutched. Sadiah smiled. Dandey noticed her watery eyes, glistening the reflection of the last purple sunrays. She looked at her brother playing with the trolley, while talking to Amisah in a language that Dandey could neither understand nor identify.

"I don't know," she said. "I was young…the only memory I have is what my mother and grandmother told me about him. He was not a very good man, but a hardworking one. My mother always said to me that all I need from a man if I want to survive is 'hardworking.' But I don't agree with her, I mean, I can be as hardworking as a man too. And we're still breathing now without him." She wiped her tears. "He was a fisherman," she added, smiling.

"Do you know how to fish?" Dandey asked, hoping to cheer up the conversation, but not sure how.

"Of course lah bah I know, but it's not easy. It depends on luck. There could be days when you catch no fish at all, and now we don't have a boat and fishing gear anymore. My uncle took them after Father passed away."

Dandey said nothing afterwards. They were quiet again for a while, watching Udin and Amisah play with the shopping trolley – so gay and carefree.

When Amisah joined them on the metal bench again, she cried, "Bang bah…five ringgit only. Don't be so stingy…Allah will bless you if you give me money."

"You didn't even share your rambutan with Sadiah," Dandey said. He was starting to get annoyed. "No, I don't have money anymore."

"Liar," Amisah said. "People like you should always have money."

"No. I'm poor too."

"At least you don't have to beg for money like us," she said.

That's true, Dandey thought.

"Bang bah...I'm still hungry…the rambutan was nothing. It's like drinking water only."

"Where are you guys going to sleep tonight?" Dandey asked, trying to maneuver the conversation. He was tired of Amisah's cries.

"At the fish market lah," Sadiah answered, "I've told you already."

"Is there a place to sleep over there? Like a shelter?"

"Yes," she said, and then looked away.

"Bang, what's your name?" Amisah asked.

"Dandey – D. A. N. D. E. Y," he spelled it and they followed his spelling in unison including Udin. Dandey felt like a teacher. He waited for them to pronounce it, but for a few seconds they were quiet, distorting their faces, struggling to imagine the letters in their heads, and how each letter combined and created a meaningful sound.

"Duh-Lee!" Amisah yelled confidently like a good student.

"It's Dandey," he corrected her, smiling.

"Dandey…" they said together.

"Amisah! Amisah! Look! Sadiah! Look!" Udin yelled, pointing at a young man who was jumping up and down. There was a young woman, taking photos of his jumping poses, and a little boy who was unwrapping a chocolate Twiggies. It was a young family: the parents were in their early twenties, and their son was about six years old. The boy stood next to his mother, whining that he couldn't unwrap his Twiggies, but his mother ignored him. The father jumped with his legs stretched open like a frog's, and flashes of camera light captured his jumping images. Dandey, the girls and Udin laughed watching the man.

"He looks so stupid!" Amisah laughed.

"Again!" The wife yelled at her husband. "Stop crying, James! You cannot see what I'm doing now, is it? I'm busy, wait!" She took another photo of her husband. The little boy kept crying, then the mother grabbed the chocolate Twiggies from her son's hands, and threw it on the ground. Dandey was shocked.

The boy continued crying, and when he wanted to retrieve his Twiggies, his father said, "James, no! It's dirty! It's trash already. We'll get you a new one. Come, let's go!" He grabbed his son's hand and dragged him along with him while talking to his wife, laughing at the photos she'd taken. The boy was still crying, but his parents ignored him. Dandey felt so angry for the boy.

Then in a split second, Udin jumped off the shopping trolley and fell, hitting the cement ground hard. Dandey was surprised, but before he could react Udin got up and ran toward the trash. He picked it up and then yelled, "Sadiah! Amisah! Look!" Smiling from ear to ear, he ran to them, screaming and laughing, with his eyes shimmering like the ripples on the ocean, holding the chocolate Twiggies high up in the air like a golden trophy, not even aware of the blood dribbling down his knees and forehead, staining his already stained shorts and torn t-shirt.

BLOGCASTER

ALEXANDER MARCOS OSIAS

BLOGOY LIVES

[BATMANONG | 1:45 AM]

It wasn't a hoax. There are hundreds of copies of the dozens of versions of these blogs stashed all around the Net if you know where to look. We'll make sure Blogoy's story gets told.

And I don't care what anyone else says – it all really started with this blog entry:

Who Knew I'd Be Worth It?

Just this morning I had breakfast with an old college batchmate and blogcast circle colleague. Seems like our blog has enough influence with the voting public to warrant a substantial fee for some announcements and considerations for a certain would-be President, and he approached me about considering accepting a bribe.

He didn't put it exactly in those terms, but let me share the details with you and let you decide. I haven't had much experience with the "real journalistic approach" for very long, so please bear with my attempt to communicate the facts clearly with you.

I'm paid to do three things:

1. Get the press releases of this candidate out on my blog.
2. Downplay any negative coverage or issues that arise regarding that candidate.
3. Ensure that none of the other candidates get any coverage on my blog.

He was very convincing. His main arguments as to why I should do it were very simple: "Everyone's doing it already" and "You're going to write about this candidate anyway". The latter bit is true – I volunteered to blog every bit of candidate gossip (and mark it as such, naturally), every scrap of candidate scandal that appears in the news, every morsel of information that filters down through the SMS chain of data and post it on this blog. Even the press releases.

So here I am. Bribed into becoming a media mouthpiece. Well, I'd better earn my pay, right? Here goes:

> **METRO MANILA** – A well-known blogcaster, Blogoy, accepted money from another well-known and once-respected blogcaster, TunaFriend, in exchange for skewing his coverage on the presidential elections.
>
> TunaFriend, claiming to represent presidential candidate Reynaldo Tambuk, handed Blogoy an ATM card as payment. Blogoy later found out that the ATM card gave him access to a BPI bank account with P30,000 in the balance.

"[It will be a] regular monthly deposit," said TunaFriend over their lunch meeting at the California Pizza Kitchen in Shangri-la Plaza. "It should increase the closer it gets to the elections."

It is unclear at this point whether or not the payments will continue after the elections.

I've attached the scans of the ATM card and the printout of the account's current balance. What do you think about the name on the ATM card? It's obviously not mine, because (for those of you who've tuned in late) I'm a guy. Male. Dude. Pare. The last name is particularly telling.

Now, I don't know if this will put our beloved candidate in hot water. <downplay on>This Blogoy is an unreliable source, after all. And where is the proof that TunaFriend really represents the candidate in question? <downplay off>

Okay I guess that's it for this month! Tune in next month when I earn my next P30K!

Comments (2):

Di ba this was that post that appeared on *The Watchful Eye* last year in April, when the elections were just beginning to boil over? When I read it I remember thinking: patay ka, Blogoy!
KidKonyo | 5:45 PM

I'd already stopped reading *The Watchful Eye* and the posts of Blogoy in particular. But when a friend forwarded me that link, I was enthralled once more.
But even then, I could only see it end in tragedy.
EDM_III | 9:27 AM

BEGINNER'S BLUNDER [KIDKONYO | 6:45 PM]

When you backread the earliest entries on his personal blog, di ba malinaw? Blogoy did not hop onto the web out to change the roiling mess that is Philippine political scene. Check this out:

Why Blogoy?

A lot of people have submitted theories regarding the significance of my name and how it reflects my personality.

Actually, it was a mistake. I was supposed to register this site as Blogboy (I know – very imaginative), but the letter 'b' sticks on this stupid keyboard and I didn't notice it till I hit 'submit'. It turns out that Blogboy has already been registered, so I decided to stick with it. I figured that when I came up with something better I could always change it.

Unfortunately I have a lot of name recall now so, I can't.

Well, I can, but I don't want to.

So I won't.

On My Own – Sort of

Moved into my family's condo in Pasig. It's near the Ortigas Metroplex, it's a bit too far from the MRT to walk, but it's cozy and I get my own room for once. Wish I could get a faster connection – I only signed up for a shared T1 connection and the regular HD movie and video feeds take forever to download.

I was really tempted to go for the dedicated connection, but I'm going to have to wait till next month. I'm getting rid of the family crutches (my monthly allowance) and getting an honest-to-God paycheck now.

Yes, I have a job! I can't tell you where it is though – blogging about work is prohibited by the contract that they make you sign – so I'm just going to have to hint at it in the future.

Now that I actually have to pay for my own food, I think I'm going to have to learn how to cook more than just pasta and soup, especially since Aileen prefers handling computers over electric stoves.

Come on Aileen

Ah, Aileen. She's more of a techie than I am – she gets this manic glow that radiates from her when she discusses her laptop and peripherals with me (most of it goes over my head, but I try to take note of the terms she repeats most often).

Like a lot of the folks at work, she held a flawed assumption that folks from the U.S. sleep around all the time like on cable. It took a while before she realized how boring and quiet my social life really was over there.

At least now she knows why I was so well-behaved over there – I was sent to the States after I almost killed a boy from a rival barkada over some stupid misunderstanding in our little corner of Parañaque (our first home in Metro Manila). I also told her about how our family split up as a result: Papa moved with me to the U.S. to make sure none of my old friends tried to contact me, while Mama went back to her family in Ilocos.

Papa eventually left me in the States when he saw I'd grown up a bit. I will love him forever for not giving up on me like mama did. He always told me Mama was the love of his life, and those cold rainy nights in Seattle spent apart from her were killing him.

I didn't understand it at the time, but on these nights when Aileen and I while the hours away talking about the darkness in our pasts and the hope we have for our future, I get some small glimpse of what their love must be like – a joyful stillness in the unjust, irrational, and sometimes dangerous place we call our home.

Speaking of dangerous places, Aileen's taking me to the shooting range tomorrow. She says her grandfather (a highly-respected former military man) could never respect a man who didn't know how to take care of himself in a fight.

Comments (2):

It's clear he was a novice to blogging and to living in Metro Manila – he drops clues to his identity right and left, believing that the Net afforded him some measure of anonymity. But all activities on the Net leave tracks.
And Metro Manila is smaller than you think.
BatManong | 2:59 AM

I concur. His posts reveal a contented, yet directionless graphic designer sharing snippets of his life with the general public.
EDM_III | 10:42 AM

A DALLIANCE WITH SENSATIONALISM

[EDM _ III | 9:31 AM]

Mere months after his foray into blogging, Blogoy and future *Watchful Eye* co-founder Bong Badong created a conspiracy site called *CounterSpin*. It was a two-man blog filled with unsubstantiated rumors and wild theories that started, peaked, and fizzled out. Unlike his later work, most of Blogoy's *CounterSpin* writings reek of sophomoric editorialism or adolescent demagoguery:

The Most Democratic Country in the World

Just the other day, I was at the Coffee Bean and Tea Leaf down the street and a foreigner (does it really matter which country?) was complaining about the state of democracy in this country. I laughed out loud when I heard his rather long rant because it reminded me of my grandfather.

He used to say that the Philippines is the most democratic country in the world. Even the dead can vote, and they do so multiple times.

I wish there were a way to stop these ghostly voters. They're obviously not very up-to-date – they keep voting the wrong people into office!

The Power of the Purse

I sometimes wonder if the widening gap between the rich and the poor is a conspiracy on the part of the elite to make bribery more viable to those of us who have been graced with the public's trust and interests.

My father is quick to point out that I am considered part of the elite – my family is well-off (some would say rich, but I've seen how the rich live and I stick by my self-assessment) and our relatives are involved in politics – but my own earning capacity is limited and I'm just not that close to my politically active kin.

My father also points out that given the oppressive unpredictability of our current institutions, it's not hard to imagine that some of my former classmates, co-workers, and blogcasting colleagues would be strongly tempted to engage in envelopmental journalism (slanted articles in exchange for cash, often in an unmarked envelope). Money could be tight, a crisis could rear its ugly head, and in a moment of weakness you are ensnared.

I hope that I'm never placed in that position. I came back from the States with so many hopes for the future of the Philippines – if someone as screwed up as I was could change his ways, surely this country can make a similar recovery.

Then again, we'd need a strong disciplinarian of a leader, and I don't think we'd like that, no matter how well-meaning the leader might be. We prefer leaders who say what we want to hear, who hand us our thirty pieces of silver before stabbing us in the back. We prefer to believe in baseless promises of freedom, security, and comfort, rather than paying the price that those luxuries demand.

TRO means Temporary Restraining Order

For those of you who haven't caught the news yet, a Makati regional trial court has issued a TRO against the Philippine Center for Investigative Journalism (PCIJ), ordering them to take down an article on their blog on the basis of personal privacy. The subject of this article – an exploration of the credentials and history of the administration's audio-visual expert Jonathan Mallorca Tengco – seems to have touched off a firestorm of media attention.

While I respect the organization's recognition for the rule of law, I find this roundabout censorship of a news agency's article offensive. Therefore, I've provided a link below where a PDF version of the article can be downloaded. I'll take it down when the TRO is lifted (or expires – which is more likely).

Download: Resident_Expert.pdf

Fellow bloggers, download this and post it on your sites. Share them with everyone (but don't forget to attribute the article properly).

Oh, for those of you who don't want to be slapped with a temporary restraining order, I've prepared the banner below. Copy it and stick it on your blogs, fellow blogcasters!

<img src="/banners/don't_TRO_me.jpg">

These posts are clearly at odds with the popular perception of Blogoy: the crusading reporter, the impartial investigator, the relentless whistleblower of last year's elections. He comes across more as an amateur pundit or a frustrated rabble-rouser.

In fact, it was his partner in rumor-peddling – Bong Badong – who first voiced concerns about their activities:

> **Spinning Out Of Control**
>
> Our days are numbered, but not due to any Orwellian organization's activities. Blogoy and I have tried to raise issues and alternative interpretations of the events that are transpiring in our country. We'd hoped to encourage open discussion, and have requested that all comments on our articles and editorials contain solid reasoning and logic or provide some measure of fact or truth.
>
> A brief sampling of the site makes it clear than these comments are few and far between. All we seem to be doing is fanning the flames of speculation.
>
> In the upcoming days we will attempt some format changes, but if the current trend continues, *CounterSpin* will have to end its online life.

But we never got to see those changes. They ceased updating the site several days later, consigned it to electronic oblivion, then rededicated themselves to following a more journalistic ethic while retaining some degree of anonymity – *Watchful Eye* was born.

The bulk of Blogoy's more professional work appeared here, alongside the posts of his three contemporaries: Bong, who established himself early as a staunch critic of the Department of Education and popular media; Jones Bridget, who claimed the arena of foreign policy and women's rights as her bailiwick, and Tunafriend, who was originally admired for his detailed reporting and the environmental slant of his writing but was later reviled and cast out of the circle.

All four members of the blog originally had personal blogsites hosted on the same server as the main news-related blog, hoping to post personal notes and insights into the preparation of each article or answer insightful questions from readers.

This practice ended soon after the following entries appeared in Blogoy's personal blogsite and on the *Watchful Eye* blogcast site respectively:

Absent Friends

Some friends of mine went missing the other week. They were real journalists, protégés of my lolo from his days with the Times. That's the reason I chose the term "blogcaster" over the more popular and more difficult to pronounce term 'blogjournalist'. Not only does blogcaster sound better – it's more accurate. There's no art in my writing, no effort in my research, no real danger in my anonymous (though factual) posts.

They told me that an informant had suddenly called for an emergency meeting scant days after their last tête-à-tête and didn't even haggle over price. I warned them that it sounded suspicious, but Erlinda scoffed at my paranoia. "Death will come for us in the night," she said with a fatalistic glint in her eye, "not from some coffee meeting with an aging bureaucrat." Louis laughed and slugged back the remainder of his beer.

Now, two days later with no responses to texts or calls, all I can do is hope for the best.

Two Journalists Murdered in Manila

The body of Louis Torreo was found in an open field near Roxas Blvd just a few hours ago. He was apparently stabbed to death and was pronounced dead on the scene. His colleague, Erlinda Chen, died twenty minutes ago at PGH from internal bleeding.

Both were reportedly investigating a story on the electronic voting booths that were summarily junked three weeks ago, necessitating the return to paper ballots.

The members of the *Watchful Eye* condemn these atrocities and urge the authorities to find the guilty and punish them.

So the members of *Watchful Eye* took steps to distance their online personas from their real lives, afraid of the consequences of their blog entries on their friends and family. They hid and purged their personal blogsites and limited their posts to articles only.

Comments (2):

Good post. Well-researched.
BatManong | 5:30 AM

Good post. *Astig*!
KidKonyo | 3:45 PM

UNMASKED **[KIDKONYO | 6:51 PM]**

Duwag ang nag-out kay Blogoy in the comment pages for *Watchful Eye*.

After going through very complicated things like IP address tracing, account hacking, and even some stalking, this guy revealed that Blogoy was Benjamin Penado Macaranas, a distant relative of President Tambuk's Chief of Staff Jose Penado.

Instead of deleting the comment, pinost nya ito:

I Am Who I Am

I'm not certain why there's a hue and cry over my identity. Yes, I am Benjamin P. Macaranas and I have made no secret of my privileged upbringing or the fact that I belong to a political family (our branch is not active politically, but that's beside the point). Part of the reason we have these personal blogs is to disclose personal information that may impact our articles but obscure them in such a way as to retain some measure of privacy.

Much of the sentiment surrounding my unmasking seems to originate from the perception that my articles are "anti-administration" and "anti-rich" and "anti-establishment". For those of you still reading, look closely and you'll note that I'm only "anti-corruption" and wholeheartedly write and fight for the good governance of this country the best way that I can.

Even rich kids want a better country.

Comments (1):

It is unlikely that Blogoy was unaware of the dangers of posting too much information on the web such as an admission of identity. Despite his professed desire for privacy in matters concerning his family and loved ones, he was quite forthcoming about himself, and many of his subsequent posts seemed obsessed with proper disclosure, especially after the traumatic accusations of being branded a fake and a traitor to the blogcasting community.
Also, please re-write your entry in English.
EDM_III | 9:45 AM

[deleted by moderator]
KidKonyo | 6:01 PM

[deleted by moderator]
KidKonyo | 3:47 PM

THE FUSE IS LIT [EDM_III | 10:30 AM]

Blogoy suffered a few weeks of ignominy, and then successfully reclaimed his reputation and respect after a series of exposés on the erosion of the integrity of traditional media organizations spearheaded by his "Who Knew I'd Be Worth It?" post.

For weeks thereafter he revealed the inner workings of several election campaigns – the early groundwork on pre-election surveys, pre-fabricated election returns, pre-stuffed replacement ballot boxes, strategic buy-offs and positioning of key Comelec personnel – complete with times and dates of meetings, the schedules of payoffs, and the personalities on either side of the exchange.

Comelec Chameleon

It is becoming difficult to keep track of which side certain Comelec officials now answer to. Take the example of Atty. Armando Juete, who has been wined and dined on no less than fourteen different occasions to date.

If frequency of visits is the measure of loyalty, then President Tambuk leads with separate visits by four different spokesmen, followed by Senator Apples Magdao with three visits by a single spokesman. Renowned actor Artemio "Art" Torrales follows with two visits by two spokesmen, and each of the remaining candidates had one visit apiece.

How can he hope to retain any semblance of independence or impartiality? How can he avoid being beholden to one or all of these parties? There is clearly one side he does not consider himself beholden to: the Philippine People.

So it falls to me. Perhaps I should visit him on our behalf. But I don't think I can match the caliber of the last spokesperson that visited – I look terrible in a miniskirt and lipstick.

Blogoy also called into the question the integrity of all other sources of news – the broadsheets, the TV channels, the radio stations:

Temptation Islands

When I was studying in the States, an Imam once told me that the "Powers That Be" have a progression of methods in dealing with agitators and troublemakers:

"First they try to trivialize you. Then they try to buy you off with sex. Then money. Then power. Failing all these, then they try to hurt you. Killing you is the final option – no one wants a martyr for a cause."

Well, we've already been officially trivialized before. I wonder if the sudden increase in attempts to personally contact us through our site are for the sex? We'd better hold out for the money – I don't want the responsibility of power, and I certainly don't want anyone hurt.

On a serious note, two friends of mine (real journalists) have shared with me the terms "envelopmental journalism" and "ATM journalism". Both of these are the derogatory terms associated with the practice of giving money – usually in an envelope or through an ATM debit card – to journalists to slant their writing to favor a particular politician, issue, or corporation.

I understand envelopes, but ATMs? Well, I guess there are benefits to that approach: they can earn interest if the journalist opts not to withdraw the hush money. They can also empty the accounts if the journalist doesn't deliver.

So the next time you find yourself taken by the portrayal of a candidate on a TV channel, or are swayed by the arguments of a persuasive radio personality, think twice.

It was not, as many of the journalists took it at the time, a blanket condemnation. Had they bothered to read all his entries, they would have realized that the institution of the free press was of particular import to Blogoy, as it dominated the content of his "professional" posts. His dogged coverage of the terrible epidemic of journalist killings in that year, as well as his advocacy for strong, honest, and professional news coverage of the political arena, earned him a reprieve from derision in select journalistic circles:

Philippines Again The Most Dangerous Spot for Journalists

The Philippines has reclaimed the number one spot as the most dangerous spot in the world for active journalism. With the deaths of two more journalists just last week, the total count for this year is 21, bringing the total journalists killed since President Tambuk's rise to power to 61, pulling further away from the record set by President Gloria Macapagal Arroyo during her term.

The Bigger Issue

I don't normally respond too directly to comments made on the blogcast articles, but the posts of news peak (whose comments, I might add, share the same IP address as TunaFriend's post-*Eye* comments) concerning the article titled "Philippines Now Most Dangerous Spot for Journalists" irk me by raising issues that, while having some merit, clearly serve the purpose of redirecting the topic of discussion away from the subject at hand.

He says:

> *Why are the so-called "Watchers", and you in particular, so taken with this elitist view of journalists? All murders pose a threat to society.*
>
> *I find this unwarranted emphasis on the deaths of journalists, as if they were better than any other citizens of the Philippines, hypocritical and smacks of a biased slant.*
>
> *If you really wanted to address the ever-growing number of journalist corpses, then write about the core issue: murder in Philippine society.*

First, I disagree with your statement that we need to address the issue of dying journalists by addressing murder in a broader sense. We have already done so by cleverly stating in our laws that murder is illegal and should be punished appropriately. What we need to do to address the "issue of journalist murders" is to investigate the murders, catch those responsible, and prosecute them to the full extent of the law.

Second, the frequency of deaths in this profession is statistically significant, indicating that there is a threat to what I consider one of the pillars of a strong democracy. For this reason alone, there should be increased calls for action. A free press must act as a watchdog on the activities of rich and poor, public servant, and citizen alike.

Third, despite your abrasive and inflammatory tone, you have a point. Perhaps there should be an investigation into why there has been an increase in murders (largely unsolved) during President Tambuk's term of office. The strict enforcement of the law is of concern to everyone, wouldn't you agree?

> *I take issue with the phrase "bringing the total journalists killed since President Tambuk's rise to power".*
>
> *What are you trying to insinuate? There is no basis in trying to establish a correlate rise in journalistic deaths with an arbitrary period that coincides with the presence of a particular politician.*

I'm insinuating nothing; I'm simply stating facts. Perhaps a better analysis of the statistics would yield better results as to the causes.

On the other hand, a president has a responsibility for law and order and candidates past and present have made it a key component of their election platforms.

This last post came somewhat ominously after President Reynaldo Tambuk's "surprise" declaration that he would run for a second term despite the clear lack of constitutionality.

COMMENTS (0):

[None]

FIRST BLOOD [BATMANONG | 2:32 AM]

This is not the final version of the links page, but I'm certain that this was the first series of links that was published on *Watchful Eye*.

All self-proclaimed experts on his career agree that Blogoy consciously avoided publishing this post to the blog, but few agree why. Some argue some family-related conspiracy, others claim an attempt to blackmail President Tambuk, and still others believe simple cowardice drove Blogoy to withhold this post from publication for months.

We may never know why the lines were crossed, and that post (clearly dated months before the Blogoy's downward spiral) aired for a day and a half on his site. Though not too many people caught it at first (due to the bandwidth problems that were plaguing the Philippines at the time), some enterprising soul managed to copy all the files on the file server, including several videos not listed on the blog entry.

Mga Putang Ina Ninyo!

My dad used to tell this joke: An American, a Frenchman, and a Filipino were stuck in a WWII foxhole. Knowing they were doomed to die, they went one by one to their deaths.

Fond of liberty and fearful of internment, the first to charge was the Frenchman, yelling, "Vive la France!"

Next was the gung-ho American, who tore into enemy fire shouting, "Long Live the U.S.A!"

Last was the Filipino, who ran into the hail of lead screaming, "Mga putang ina ninyo!" ("All your mothers are whores!")

That's how I feel right now. Enjoy, everyone, enjoy.

Download: Candidate Scandal 1 – Bathroom Break
Download: Candidate Scandal 2 – Boardroom Balling
Download: Candidate Scandal 3 – Hallway Happenings
Download: Candidate Scandal 4 – Stairway to Heaven
Download: Candidate Scandal 5 – Landing Letdown
Download: Candidate Scandal 6 – Faulty Tower

I certainly hope you enjoyed your visit to our offices, Candidate Tambuk and friends. Please do bring your wife next time, we'd love to meet her too.

It was not long after this post became widely available that the end came for Blogoy and the rest of his colleagues.

Comments (0):

[None]

FEET OF COLD CLAY [KIDKONYO | 6:58 PM]

Two days after the accidental publication of the cheekily titled "Election Scandal", the following entry appeared on the blog:

> **Should We Stay Or Should We Go?**
>
> We three, the remaining Watchers, have been debating whether or not to go on hiatus until after the elections. Some of our recent reports have apparently angered several powerful individuals, and we now fear for our lives.
>
> The more sarcastic segment of our reading public may scoff at my fear, with their flawed view of me and my family's influence in the political world. Allow me to short-circuit the upcoming debate to remind you all: the campaign proper has already turned violent, with several candidates injured and one killed.
>
> Is this the battle where we retreat to fight another day, or the one where we stand our ground? In my youth, I wouldn't have hesitated and jumped into the fray with a smile and a snarl.
>
> Now, I look around at the people I love and realize how much I stand to lose if I continue.

Less than a week later, the posts on *Watchful Eye* slowed to a trickle. The reports that did come out were factual, but lacked teeth. The members of the first blogcaster circle had balked and backed down – but only halfway.

They had been asked to do two things – stop writing their entries, and take their blog off the web with all their past entries, links and comments. They had complied with the first demand, but had omitted the second.

Several anonymous demands were posted in the comments of the latest entries. They went unanswered for several days.

Then the murders began.

The following entries appeared on the *Watchful Eye* public site in rapid succession:

Bong Badong Murdered in Greenhills

Arnel Lipunan, Jr. was gunned down by a pair of assassins on a motorcycle last Tuesday night. He was returning from the Greenhills Shopping Center to his home, braving the rush hour traffic, when an electric blue motorcycle carrying two helmeted individuals stopped beside his vehicle and emptied a clip of 9mm rounds into the driver's side of his vehicle.

Arnel Lipunan, known to many as Bong Badong, head of the blogcasting circle *Watchful Eye*, died instantly when the first bullet entered his skull.

Jones Bridget Murdered in Quezon City

They're after us. The unidentified woman whose body was found along N. Domingo early last Thursday morning was identified by her family this morning. She was Camilla Martirez, known to people who frequent this site as Jones Bridget, and she was a good friend.

She was apparently accidentally run over by a beat-up Toyota Innova driven by a fifty-year old man named Tristan Macaraeg. According to witnesses, she was thrown, with her hands and feet bound, in front of the unsuspecting Macaraeg's vehicle.

I guess I'm next.

Farewell to Tuna

All the eyes have closed but mine. John Cruzado, once known on this blogcast circle as TunaFriend, fell from the balcony of his brand new condo while entertaining guests.

It's interesting to see that he overcame his life-long fear of heights and spent the last moments of his life "horsing around along the edge of the balcony" when he slipped and fell, according to friends present.

Poor John. He should've been more discerning in his choice of friends.

No doubt Blogoy's lineage kept him safe for a few weeks, and the sudden inactivity of the site seemed to indicate that the once-fearless Blogoy had been cowed.

COMMENTS (3):

[deleted by moderator]
EDM_III | 9:45 AM

[deleted by moderator]
KidKonyo | 5:01 PM

Behave. Final warning.
BatManong | 4:07 AM

RIPOSTE [EDM _ III | 10:13 AM]

The silence was broken by a damning near-encyclopedic summary of then-President Tambuk's illegal activities, indexed and hyperlinked, on a separate site.

The Truth – Hijacking an Election

President Tambuk is unwilling to let go of his Presidency and will do anything to hold on to it and has done an admirable job of it.

It started early in his campaign, during his visits to the provinces of Pampanga and Lanao del Sur and the ARMM. Considered strongholds of his fiercest competitor, Antonia de la Cruz, he lavished time and money taken from various sources (See **The Truth – Filling the War Chest**) and courted key people in those positions.

The extent of such campaigning is difficult to quantify, given the subsequent manipulation of the supposedly independent polls conducted by Trendfinders, the source of poll interpreting bodies like PulsePhilippines and Social Metrics Matrix (See **The Truth – Salting the Polltakers**).

This important task was entrusted to Illustrio Tambuk, a close cousin of President Tambuk's and was no doubt undertaken to help justify one or more upsets in these provinces. Illustrio and his organization were efficient and effective, if somewhat overzealous in their work – a startling average of 56% to 69% support for President Tambuk in these areas triggered suspicions, poll falsification, and mass rallies for Ms. De la Cruz in those same provinces (events that were subsequently forgotten, after newer election-related scandals arose).

At the same time that this was happening, President Tambuk's wife and brother-in-law were busy at the clan's printing house, generating a large supply of pre-printed, pre-answered, and pre-approved ballot forms for each of the precincts, municipalities, cities, and provinces identified as crucial for a "clear mandate from the people" (For samples of each form, see **The Truth – Falsified Election Documents**).

In most areas, these falsified ballots replaced the real ballots after the polls had closed, though in certain areas (most notably Pampanga, Lanao del Sur, and ARMM) these substitutions were done after the elections to corroborate the falsified numbers announced during the count at the Batasan, and the falsified Certificates of Canvass (COCs) that replaced the actual COCs.

The control of election operations was not solely a family affair, however, as two other operators with their own organizations were used to ensure victory: one within Comelec, and one within NAMFREL. A documentary video of the count and announcing of results made with the aid of concerned members of the Congress and Senate through a series of smuggled in digital cameras clearly shows members of this organization reading out, writing down, or otherwise misrepresenting key tallies at the Batasan (See the video links at **The Truth – The New Math**). Not everyone shown committing election fraud did so willingly – some were coerced.

In charge of this operation was Efren Halcon, former AFP chief and current intelligence advisor to President Tambuk. Interviews and frank admissions from some of his closest lieutenants to this blogcaster revealed that nothing was sacred – blackmail, kidnapping, rape, and murder were all used in securing the obedience or silence of key personalities in Comelec, NAMFREL, and the news media. Not even relatives of members of the AFP were spared their attention.

It is likely that Blogoy stepped out from under the protective aegis of his family because of what happened to his girlfriend Aileen Dimagiba Lorenzo.

Fifteen days after President Tambuk was declared the winner of the elections, and nine days after Blogoy's "Showdown in the Batasan" entry, Aileen disappeared from work at 3:00 pm and never returned. In a manner similar to the deaths of his friends Louis Torreo and Erlinda Chen, she was lured to a supposed meeting with her immediate superior at the Sulo Hotel, was kidnapped, abused, then set free. Found wandering the streets of Quezon City, she was rushed to St. Luke's by her family where she died of internal injuries several days later.

Immediately after her funeral – which Blogoy was prohibited from attending by the venerable patriarch of the Dimagiba family, General Arturo Dimagiba – the renewed attack on the Tambuk campaign appeared. The loss of any sense of journalistic distance is clearly evident, but as everyone knows, the findings were eventually proven accurate.

Comments (3):

Not all the links work.
KidKonyo | 5:05 PM

Of course not. They ceased to work when the original servers were taken offline.
EDM_III | 9:49 AM

It would've better if you'd included them.
KidKonyo | 3:27 PM

I'm turning off the comments.
BatManong | 4:07 AM

FINALE [BATMANONG | 2:31 AM]

The details of Blogoy's extrajudicial execution are a matter of public record and are available for download from most independent news sites. The video clip that details his last five minutes on earth, while reviled by many modern blogcasters, is quite familiar – it is a staple of all college level courses in blogjournalism, and is often a part of blogcaster circle orientation kits.

Benjamin P. Macaranas's legacy to his family was one of love and thoughtfulness, one that will be forever cherished by those of us who knew him. But I am proudest of his legacy to the country – a record of his life and death as the country's first true blogcaster.

And so I leave you with this: the last blog of the last member of the *Watchful Eye* blogcaster circle, Blogoy.

Adios Patria Adorada

Three black Pajeros just rolled into the ground floor parking lot. I couldn't get a clean still on the security webcams, but the license plates are probably stolen anyway. They're here for me, unless I'm fortunate enough to be mistaken.

To my family, I wish I had more time to make you proud of me.

To my friends from the Paterno Memorial Fund – I hope you got the donations I made in the name of Louis and Erlinda. You can thank our re-elected President Tambuk.

To my esteemed colleagues and respected journalists – I've e-mailed the zipped contents of my files to you, and sent other copies to my relatives in Canada, Norway, France and the U.S.

And last but not least, to my dearest Aileen – wait a little longer, I'll be with you soon.

My name is Benjamin P. Macaranas.

If you don't hear from me again, keep my words alive.

AUTO-REJECTION: AN OUTRO

NIN HARRIS

All of the Bunian Empress's lizard bomohs, and all of her crocodile-men, could not make a spell strong enough to get rid of two lumps. 1.5 centimeters in diameter, perfectly shaped and coyly lodged beneath fat and tissue. No, the only thing that would work would be the severing of your head from your body, and learning how to pickle yourself like any good penanggalan would.

You auto-rejected yourself from communities, from relationships, from jobs that you were sure were going to rob you of your light and your capacity for joy. And now, it seemed as though your body has decided to auto-reject you from life. The light and joy had left years ago.

This was going to be a tale about you auto-rejecting yourself from love, but that is the same thing, is it not? At least the metaphysical poets that you read in college with all of their Occidental phlegm and authority would have you believe that. You either had love, or you had death. To live meant to be exposed to the possibility of acceptance, and therefore rejection. To auto-reject yourself from one, meant to auto-reject yourself from another. Besides, you've always been more terrified of acceptance and all that would entail.

All of the Empress's owl-sisters, all of the djinns of the earth, could not stitch your sinew and tissue back together again. All of the owl-sisters with their nightly ululations, male entrails spilled in a bloody trail in mimicry of the penanggalan's delicately vinegared coils, could not remove the tumor. Surgeons could. Or would. But in your head, the denial had already occurred. There was no way this was going to be benign. The same way there was no way you were going to get that copywriting job at that advertising firm, the same way there was no way Vinod was for real. You had auto-rejected yourself from all possibilities.

Auto-rejecting from the possibility of living past another birthday was therefore a fitting outro for the LP of your life.

X

If you can hear them, it is beyond belief that anyone could stay up after midnight in Kuala Lumpur without being aware of the unloving songs the owl-sisters sing. You have never been able not to hear their songs. Not the loudest punk-rock albums, not even the hardcore screamo masterpieces that caused your uncles to howl at you to keep the volume down. Not meditation. Not masturbation. Nothing could stop you from hearing the music of the penanggalans since you hit puberty.

X

You were born here, and you grew up in Brickfields, poised in-between the gentrification, and the run-down apartments pushed further back by encroaching structures of glass and steel. You walked to college past rank trashcans close by KL Sentral to get to your A-Level classes, where the disconnect between learning the literatures of the Commonwealth and the reality of where you lived became a source of constant precocious amusement for you and your classmates. You lived with your uncles and your siblings because your mother had murdered your father. You lived with your uncles who had trapped your ravaging mother with jampi and pineapple skins.

Your siblings have all moved to other, more affordable cities. You live in an apartment complex so grimly different from the luxury condominium projects near Pantai that the name "condominium", emblazoned on a dirt-grimed banner hung between posts at the entrance, is a mockery of the inhabitants. Those inhabitants drag themselves out of bed every morning to perform their ablutions, their prayers, and to move about doing the jobs that rarely get filmed or advertised. Like you, as you silently walk every morning toward the small photocopying and design business run by your uncles, adjacent to your teenhood home.

You moved out to return to your uncles the privacy they gave up to look after your siblings and you, ignoring the sidelong glances and the gossip, to raise a family as best they could. You spend every day of your life with them. You throw yourself into an existence in which you do everything that needs to be done in a family business, from the typesetting to the balancing of the books, to playing Chinese Checkers with the uncles at coffee break.

The irony of living a life in which you clear-sightedly believe in horrors is that you cannot bring yourself to believe in everyday wonders, apart from your gentle uncles. It was fine to believe that the penanggalan lurked in the trashcans behind your apartment complex for example, even though the penanggalan were mostly fastidious horrors, and it was logically hard to believe they would sleep there at all. It was fine to believe that a crocodile-man actually lurked in the moss-murked swimming pool in your complex, so dank that no one actually swims there apart from you.

The crocodile-man does occasionally swim lazy laps next to you while you try to ignore the scaled tail that coyly grazes your legs. This is why you should never swim at dusk, but you've never been able to obey such edicts. Nor are you able to observe other injunctions. It was easier to believe that if you were foolhardy enough to want to eat ice kacang after midnight at a certain roadside stall you should never look over your shoulder if there is a soft blowing in your ear. It was easier to believe these things because you could see them, feel them, hear them. It was not so easy to believe in a more conventional afterlife, or in a more conventional love.

X

There are other reasons why the owl-sisters do not harm you. There is a reason why you can see them, and hear them. There is a reason why the penanggalans leave you alone. They don't tell you this, do they? That penanggalans had children, that some of those children survived, that the call of the blood reaches out to them. Because penanggalans were humans, or are humans, and detaching your head from your body is a secret that was passed down to you, along with an extensive knowledge of pickling. You could believe in all of those things. Easily. What you could not believe in was the ability of human consciousness to survive the death of the body. That there were other forms of life there was no doubt. But one would always be translated beyond recognition. And there it was.

The incommensurability of one's belief in horrors and one's disbelief in wonders. Everyday wonders. Like friendship. Like acceptance, like Vinod actually returning your interest.

No, the time for that was past, many years ago. Many years ago beyond count.

You were quite sure that being descended from a penanggalan meant that you were also an erotomaniac. That was how it always started. You fall in love, you are disappointed because it was all in your head. This disappointment transmutes in your head, turning into a jilting, an actionable slight. You start making unholy pacts. You are translated, you start growing claws and fangs. Drag out entrails from the husk of your body and sing your long, lonesome, ululating song at 3am, because you always, always fall in love with your prey, when you are not feasting on the afterbirth of unfortunate mothers.

This holds true even if you marry your prey, and then discover that they are on the verge of divorcing you.

This is how you became an orphan, after all.

You have two options, really. You could wait for the biopsy report, or you could give in to the imperative of your blood. To invoke, to transform, to pull, to draw in, to be consumed, and then to consume. One could say this was predestined from the moment you walked into the bedroom where your mother's floating head was making a meal out of the remains of your father's mutilated body.

Or, you could wait for the rejection slip from the surgeon.

You could wait to be told you were going to be given another chance to self-reject at friendship, at love, at jobs. At happiness. To have another ten or twenty years of being a reject and sad fuck-up, incapable of aspiring to more than this life by the river, and pining after a man who has barely spoken 10 sentences to you in all of the time that you have known him.

Because you belonged to the night and all of its monstrosities, because you were trash by inheritance and by circumstance, you are deemed trash, even though, like all potential penanggalans, you are excessively fastidious and use antibacterial soap on everything.

The trashcan is a metaphor, you think. There was no earthly way midwives who turn into penanggalans would sleep in trashcans.

X

If the trashcan is a metaphor, then Vinod is a plot device.

You learned about plot devices in college, and later, during overpriced writing courses you took to compensate for the fact that you could not afford university fees. You tell yourself this to convince yourself that what you felt was not love, that it was a mere frisson. When you think about him, you can hear in your head the song the penanggalan sing when they're trying to win you over to their camp. *He will only hurt you, maim you, put his mark upon you.* They sing this song every time you walk past the trash cans lining the outside of your apartment complex, the pungent smell of the refuse of multiple apartments hitting your nose as you step down from the bus that stops in front of the guardhouse at 11:45pm.

Vinod is a plot device like Jeremy before him, and Ramli before that. All of your unrequited loves, all of your potential victims, rescued from meeting the fate one meets upon falling in love with someone descended from a waking horror. You convince yourself you are doing the right thing, even if Vinod's voice and his dark, hurt eyes follow your thoughts like a pet jaguar you never knew you had. One you would want to keep and cherish for all of the years of your joint existence. Because his eyes are as old and as wild as your soul, as the songs you hear at 3am. Because he's been a haunting at the back of your mind for over a decade.

You've already started keeping bottles of vinegar in your kitchen just in case, just in case you decide one day to take that path.

Be immortal like us, the penanggalan sing to you in their nocturnal ululations. You will not die, you will fly, and when the feeding is done, there will be starsong to imbibe, there are owl-sisters who will dance with you, because the condemned will always flock together. If you learn to fly high enough and to keep your entrails untangled, if your breath remains vinegary sweet, you will be allowed to reach the floating wooden palaces of the Bunian Empire. You will enjoy the sweetness of blood and the savor of flesh, and you will be young forever. Perhaps the Empress will recruit you to her army, and you will live in the skies, transformed into an apsara. Perhaps you will even be appointed as a laksamana someday. It is a beautiful story. A far more beautiful story than the reality of medical tests, and yet more tests. It seems far more feasible in your grief, than the possibility of driving yourself to and fro from chemotherapy because your uncles are too old and frail. Everyone else who loved you has gone away. It seems more feasible than succumbing to surgery and radiation while drowning in unleavened solitude.

Love is a beautiful story too. It is one you croon to yourself as a fairytale of sorts, to keep out the darkness, to have your mind ignoring the smell of the refuse piling up behind your apartment building, of the roaches that inhabit the dark when the fluorescent lights go out. The roaches that are part of the unseen army that plagues your nights and the edges of your consciousness.

X

You write this down two tables away from where he is laughing with his friends, insensible to your presence, for you are stealthy in your perpetual mortification caused by agonies of love-feelings. When Vinod laughs, his face is like a lamp that someone suddenly turned on. It offsets his grim sobriety on other occasions. The contrast is intoxicating. It draws you, every time you are in the same space. It makes you feel like an unwilling stalker. It makes you wonder if there is a line that normal people cross. But you are far from normal and you know that. The light that shines from his face is far more intoxicating than the promise of starsong, and of the sticky sweetness of afterbirth. You could so easily draw that light from his face with a penanggalan's elongated tongue. That light could bring you to the singing stars. Was that why your mother made such a thorough meal of your father?

You contemplate the painful reality of cancer versus the eternal exquisite torment of a career of murder and pickling your entrails. You would only choose the best, of course. You have splurged on bottles of apple cider vinegar, and white wine vinegar. Both types were lightly astringent and not unpleasant. For another hundred years or so you can walk upon this earth as predator, not prey. You did not have to sleep in a trashcan, not when you would be in the court of the Bunian Empress.

You write this to avoid looking at the blunt, sure lines of his face, so familiar and yet so alien. You think of all of the things you might have said to him, might have done to make it all better, to turn it all normal. You think of all of the ways you have avoided further contact, avoiding his face, avoiding his eyes, avoiding all memory of shared hopes and dreams.

Once upon a sliver of far-too-distant time, his eyes had been voluntarily on yours, and everything could have been so different had you not auto-rejected yourself from the unfamiliar, from the risk of exposure and failure.

You slap the cover of your tablet shut and pay your bill. You walk back into the dank and pungent night. You are far from normal, but you are not, you think, a murderer. You were raised by two men who loved each other very much, and who taught you that enduring love exists in this world, and that sacrifice was a part of love.

You auto-reject yourself from immortality to keep the light glowing in his eyes.

Because of course, that is what you would do. Because the metaphysical poets have taught you well.

LIFE/AFTER

FRANCIS PAOLO QUINA

So, I have to write. One of us all has to write, if this is going to get told.
– Julio Cortázar, *Blow-Up*

Teodoro had heard that old saying about dying so often, the one that claims that at the moment of death a person's entire life flashes before his eyes, that he expected it not to be true – just another piece of superstitious nonsense that had no basis in scientific fact. In a perverse way, it was good that he was jaded in that respect, for it was one less thing he was disappointed about as he was swept off his feet by the wall of loose earth and debris that had once been the hills around the city. He was crushed to death immediately by what remained of a tree, whose now-dead roots had once delicately held together everything that it rode down the hill.

He was blood and sinewy muscles and veins, no longer a man, and the earth welcomed him easily that way. He seeped through the mud; he was one with it, organic and not an inert object like a rock. In just under a minute he was gone, along with half of the small city that stood at the foot of the hills for nearly twenty years.

Teodoro had gone there two years earlier to serve as a doctor in the small hospital that serviced the city. Buried in the earth, his final thoughts were not about his life. Instead, he envisioned a future-time, not far from now, when new life rose on top of the ruins of the small city.

A root – I will be one of its many roots.

Think of the world, how time makes it so predictable – order to disorder, life to trash – now imagine how it would look if time stopped moving forward toward disorder. Imagine instead, all energy remaining as it is in this moment. Raindrops, which were falling moments before, now remain suspended in the air, like a million tiny jewels shining against the sky. The last inch of earth from the hills has yet to rest and settle over the remains of the small city.

Underneath the earth, horrified faces lie frozen in that final, panic-filled moment of death. There is nothing calm and soothing about these faces of the dead and dying. Among them, Teodoro has that great notion of being a root of new lives in his mind, a snapshot of one person's attempt to make meaning out of tragedy.

Now imagine time, that great, unnamed villain, the unimpeachable tyrant of all narrative, pulling back, moving toward order instead of chaos. The raindrops now slowly, then quickly rise to the heavens. From puddles in the ground, water separates from dirt and forms into droplets that launch upward, like a million bullets being fired by the earth to heaven.

As quickly as the hills around the small city rushed down in a tide of mud to sweep it off the face of the earth, it rushed back up to its place, holding together tenuously. Houses and vehicles, dislodged during the landslide, are thrown back to where they belonged.

People are returned to their respective lives. The school teacher is back in front of the classroom, going on and on about sine and cosine, then going off on tangents. The street vendor is back with his wares, waiting for the school to open its gate and feed the children his sweets. And the town doctor is back in his makeshift clinic, tending to a sick child.

All around the small city, life comes back. People are undoing the final moments of their lives. A mother's hand swings away from the cheeks of her daughter, her regret disappearing with it. A pickpocket slides a wallet into a man's back pocket, his relief disappearing with it. Teodoro picks up the mobile phone he had set down before and a conversation begins where it ended. He took back the words he had said, climbing back up to his lips and into that secret place where they came from.

In another part of the country, a tide of people pulls back instead of pushes. An avalanche of bodies is undone and old ladies, who were trampled to death, get back up on their feet and wait for the time for them to come home. In another part of the country, an oil tanker maneuvers successfully away from disaster, the breach in its hull repairs itself as if it were organic, like skin.

All over, deeds done were undone. An ungrateful son takes back a punch thrown at his elderly father. An ice pick stuck into a man's side is pulled out, his cellular phone returned. A man is dug out of the cemetery, brought to a funeral home, displayed there and visited by friends and family. He is brought to the hospital a few days later, then rushed by ambulance and brought into a crushed car sticking out from under a ten-wheeler truck in EDSA.

Comic politicians look more ridiculous when they take back their accusations and don't present their witnesses and evidence to ravenous reporters. Newspapers are taken out of trash cans, used to wrap tuyo, and then returned to newsstands. From there, they are taken to printing presses to be unprinted.

Printing press raids happen only because authorities have to return sequestered items. Emergencies come and go; coup plots materialize out of thin air and disappear into thin air. Bombs violently form in abandoned corners and are later picked up by shadowy men. Residents displaced by conflicts, who were running away from their homes, now back up and return. Soldiers and rebels both retreat to their lines, as bullets fly off bodies; skin mends and panic fast fades away.

Teodoro, had he been aware of this change in direction of time's arrow, would have remembered *entropy* from a class in Physics. He would have understood that the universe was finally ending, that after trillions and trillions of years expanding out from that mysterious zero point of creation, it had reached its elastic limit and was now collapsing into itself.

The sun which had risen from the east was now setting there; dawn was now dusk, and death had become birth. Teodoro moved back through many days in the small city, looking after the sick and the forgotten. Days when he could only watch as a dead child came back to a diseased life without medication. Days when the sound of gunfire, long gone, returned; when bullets lost among trees, and disappeared bodies were found and returned to their rightful places. Days when revolutionaries he had treated in subterfuge, who had died in combat, returned; still not triumphant. Military men who terrorized the small city's residents, who looked at him suspiciously, questioned him, left and went back to their bases. Cold empty shells jumped back into firearm chambers and filled with gunpowder and shrapnel with a spark of fire.

In the streets of the capital, dispersed rallies reformed chaotically. Militants soaked in water were dried with the aid of a fire truck. In one rally, the cut in one man's left arm bled again, but a riot policeman's night stick uncut him. They desisted, backed down and he and his comrades returned to campus.

Teodoro packs his things and leaves the small city. He takes back his last goodbye to his mother, and on the other end of the line, her mother's tears slowly roll up her cheek, to the corners of her eyes and straight into her tear ducts; his father's clenched fist relaxed at the sound of his voice, the conviction going, going, gone.

His friends took back their heartfelt expressions of fear, their warnings that moving so far away from Manila was a mistake. Not only was there no money to make, that the small city he was moving to was only a city in name, that it was still the boondocks.

As the bus, and then the ship, made its way back to Manila, hope came back to him. He came home to a silent house in the dead of night, his parents unaware that he would ever run away. He gave back his medical license. He erased his answers from his medical board examinations. He went back to school. His professors took back their lectures, confiscated answers and grades. Teodoro sat in front of his computer for hours erasing papers and reports. The official names of body parts he lost slowly with the efficiency he memorized them.

Moving farther back, lost loves returned, only to fade away into anonymity or chaste friendship. Janine, his first fuck. Anna, his first real girlfriend. Maybelle, the girl he could never have. Comforting fictions in Teodoro's memory revealed themselves to be lies. Acts of kindness and love turn out to be abuse. A kindly, friendly old priest's touch, which he remembers with warmth, were a pedophile's reptilian caresses.

Even moving backward, time is unrepentant. It obliterates sadness as well as bliss, terror as well as comfort, in equal measure.

His eyesight fails him slowly, his ability to speak disappears, and he is a fragile child, incapable of doing anything until that time when he is taken to the hospital and with feet first, is sucked into his mother's body, where for nine months, he began, like time, like the universe, to fold into himself – organ by organ, cell by cell.

A people's peaceful revolution never happened and a dictator is reinstated into the presidency. A world war never happens and Manila is restored to it former glory. In Bagumbayan, a small man gets up from the ground, the bullets from the firing squad flying out of his body. He returns to his cell in Intramuros. Ships from Europe sail out of the docks.

Churches were taken down, as they were built, slowly with blood and sweat. Blood shed is unshed, returned to veins from a cup of wine. The sign of the cross is undone. A Portuguese man returns to Spain from a long voyage to what is now to the world undiscovered territory, and sits alone in a tavern.

In the place where Teodoro died, four hundreds years ago, a small town flourishes.

FLOWERS FOR KK

M. SHANMUGHALINGAM

I have been dying inside for eight years. Yet my three-quarters dead body is sitting at the funeral of my formerly handsome late husband. I use my handkerchief, not to wipe away, but to hide how few tears I have left. Almost all have been used up in my eight years of marriage. Another woman beside me is wailing away. I feel betrayed twice: first, by my late husband, Kanagaretnam, alias King Kana or 'KK' to family and friends, and second, by my younger sister, Thangachi.

Whose treachery was worse?

The temple priest places camphor and sandalwood fragranced joss sticks in a copper incense holder. Then, on a large silver tray strewn with white jasmine and red rose petals, he sprinkles rosewater. He gestures to Thangachi to place this at the foot of the dark brown and gold-lined timber coffin. The wind coming through the main door blows the smoke from the joss sticks. Light gray ash smears the green and white mosaic floor. Some sticks to Thangachi's hands, which are wet with her tears. The fragrance of flowers, especially the sweet scents of frangipani and white jasmine from the wreaths, pervade the house.

Thangachi continues weeping. I spread my handkerchief to hide my face even more as her wailing reaches a crescendo.

There are many tributes, from words to flowers, for King Kana from relatives, friends, colleagues, and staff. A tall young man says, "Mrs. Kana, Chief KK helped to arrange a housing loan for my first home. I will always be grateful to him."

I hear two older men standing opposite me agreeing with each other as to what a capable man he was. They also mention that he was so strict that his finance division shone as the most disciplined and efficient in the whole department in all the country. The group from the office went on as to how it won several best service awards because of him. I shake my head, thinking they don't know what I have gone through all these years.

I never got to talk back or even just chat much with KK because he said he knew all the answers to everything I needed to know. But as soon as our relatives and friends leave I can have more than a word with Thangachi. I have enough words left to make up for my lack of tears.

As mourners and temple elders chant the religious songs, I hear one chant which soothes my soul: "O namo namo namo O namo namo namo …"

It was sung at Papa's funeral. How I wept. One second our papa was there and the next he was gone. "Our Papa is no more," I sobbed. My psychologist friend says that my wailing at Papa's funeral had a very useful purpose. My pent-up emotions and grief were released in one go. If the steam from the boiling kettle is not allowed a spout to escape from, it may explode later. But here, beside King Kana's corpse, instead of the release of weeping I retreat even deeper into my silence than when he was alive. Since I am too numb and stunned to weep, will I explode later?

Thangachi watch out, I say to myself.

I lower my handkerchief to stare at Thangachi. I recall the November evening of dark clouds and thunder a year ago when King Kana pointed his forefinger. "Indra, you have been childless for so long."

He said "you" and not "we". Our neighbor, Katijah, says it's rude to point with your forefinger, but I didn't dare remind him of that.

I had just served KK his evening tea: Ceylon, strong with freshly boiled milk and one teaspoon of honey, accompanied by kolukatai. KK claimed that every cup of tea served must go with one sweet delicacy. This was how his mother used to serve his father and him. That evening the gula Melaka, brown sugar from my freshly steamed kolukatai, was trickling down his wrist. We were both seated alone in the sitting room. He, spread out on the sofa, arms resting on his favorite 'Made in England' white-linen covered cushion from Robinsons, and I on my brown rattan chair, with my self-embroidered beige cushion. I said nothing.

"I must do something," he continued, while jabbing the cushion.

Now it was "I", not "you" or "we". It was him or me, him against me. So I remained silent.

"You know our custom."

"Which one?" I asked, my arms folded.

"You know – the one where the husband marries the childless wife's single sister."

"Oh that one," I said, trying to sound casual. "I thought the wife had to die first before the husband re-married?"

The previous evening, standing at my bedroom window after my evening shower, admiring the thick bushes of pink and white bougainvillea, I overheard KK in the garden, talking to Thangachi, on one of her many visits. He had just come home from our Kuala

Lumpur Book Club Library. I couldn't hear everything they said. He mentioned something about a date between the 7th and 10th of December as a good time for marriages according to our Hindu calendar. Silly me. I thought Thangachi was going to surprise me with some good news. I moved behind the curtain so as not to be spotted. I heard them discussing whether second marriages can be as grand, or even grander, than first ones.

"Not necessarily," he continued later with gritted teeth, while staring at me. "If she has not been productive for many years that's some kind of death. It's your duty to bear children."

Back in the sitting room, he hit our wooden table with his clenched fist, making the teaspoons jump and clatter on the saucer. I didn't jump like the teaspoons; I was used to KK's hard-fist banging acts. However, I felt a low punch to my stomach.

"So although I am not missing, I am still presumed dead?" I asked. Sarcasm gave me some consolation.

He wagged his forefinger. "From Alaska and Bhutan to China and India, from the Apache to the Sioux Red Indians to the Swazi in Africa they have been practicing these, what they call 'soror'-something. Oh yes, 'sororate' marriages. Why should we in Malaya stick out as ignorant exceptions?"

He didn't know that after overhearing him discuss his plans with Thangachi I had gone over to our library while he was at the club later that afternoon. The library assistant said she hadn't had time to replace the reference books that KK had pored over. I collapsed into the same chair he had sat on earlier, perspiring in spite of the ceiling fan beating the air at maximum speed. I was thrilled to read that the same books also said that what were called levirate marriages were practiced by the Hindu Bania caste and in Punjab and Haryana.

As I read, I was reminded that this lover of English things had forgotten what the Irish nuns in our convent had taught us. That when Arthur, Prince of Wales died, his widow, Catherine of Aragon married his younger brother, the future Henry VIII. When Prince Albert died, his fiancée Mary married his younger brother, the future George V. I could well imagine how KK would have reacted if I reminded him of all this, so I decided yet again that I was better off keeping dumb voluntarily and saving whatever was left of my shrinking face. People with tempers have a way of making us frightened, most of the time.

As if he was reading my thoughts, KK flung his cup, with hot tea still inside, against the show-case where our wedding portrait and other photos were displayed. Raising his voice, which he did whenever his argument was weak, he said, "It's your fault that I have to marry Thangachi. She should bring hope, like our sacred lotus filled with fertility to overcome your bad karma!"

As I wiped the tea from our wedding portrait I saw a smiling bride of seven years past, with large eyes, black wavy hair pinned with white jasmine, and a glow of much hope all over her face.

I was reminded of one of Aesop's many fables Amma told us. This is the one where the wolf accuses the lamb of muddying the water, although the lamb is drinking downstream and in no way could dirty the upstream water the wolf is drinking.

In the early days it was just Thangachi, me, and Amma and Papa. Amma still did all the cooking at home, although we were both teenagers, as she loved preparing all our favorite food. The kitchen was her queendom and I felt like an intruder if I lingered there for too long. Because Amma had marked her territory firmly I told Thangachi that we should retreat into branches of domestic science that did not overlap with Amma's. I became busy with sewing, embroidery, and an area of cooking that had required my use of the kitchen only for short and off-peak kitchen periods.

I made what Amma said was the best kolukatai. I also baked cakes in various shapes and colors, which were as elaborate as my embroidery. As a Libran, I had chosen harmony and peace over conflict. However, Thangachi had said, "Acca, unlike you, I will advance. Why can't we have two tigresses in our kitchen mountain, since the older one looks tired lately?"

She had done so, not only whenever Amma was out of it, but had stayed on whenever Amma was too busy to notice. Yes, Thangachi, with her childlike smile, was aggressive and impatient - such a contrast to me. She would be ideal for any young ambitious man, so I couldn't understand why she would be happy to barge into my home to be a second wife to KK, whose good looks could not overshadow his dark and violent side.

When Papa brought home bangles and other nice things for us, Amma and I had the first choice before Thangachi took her turn.

"I know you are Papa's favorite," she said.

"I only happen to be older than you, that's all," I replied. I handed her all the bangles Papa had given me, but she continued to sulk.

"We are keeping it within the family," KK said, as he finally noticed my reddened eyes.

I wanted to ask if all the world's darkest secrets weren't kept within families. Aren't most wounds caused by ourselves, or within families? But I remained mute.

The malligai in my vase had wilted. My kolukatai bypassed his heart to reach his stomach, which he was stroking. I had caught him more than once pretending to stroke his stomach, as he felt it was more manly to show prosperity than chest pain. The dark clouds outside were followed by lightning, thunder, and rain. In Malaya, I'm told, we have more lightning than most other countries because of the many tailings from our tin mining, buried in our soil.

Suddenly I recalled something that Thangachi had said; it finally made sense. I was cooking KK's dinner one evening, before KK dropped his atomic bomb on me. Thangachi had joined me in the kitchen, without being invited, asserting among other things her traditional rights as my sister. Out of nowhere she said, "Remember our unlucky aunty, PPP, 'Poor Pitiful Punitham'? They called her that because her first bed was barren. Her husband had married her sister who produced two kids from the second bed."

I slumped on the nearest stool in my kitchen. Thangachi took over my cooking. I had hoped that it would never happen to me. "Oh Lord Ganesha, let me never be the one to be accused of sleeping on a barren bed," I had prayed. Yet now my worst fear had come true.

Among the difficult things about life with KK was accompanying him to official dinners, weddings, or even to our temple on Fridays, which I didn't enjoy at all, unlike other women who were blessed with un-bossy husbands and loved dressing up. In the longest minutes before we left our home, KK often appeared all dressed up, and would push our bedroom door wide open before I was ready, place his heavy wooden armchair at the entrance, sitting cross-legged while making me turn around to check if my face and neck were evenly layered with talcum powder.

"No white patches to be seen, hair bun neatly clasped in black hairpin and black hair net, without any strand of stray hair jutting out, kondai placed not too high, slightly low almost touching the back, just above your choli saree blouse." I can still hear his instructions in my head.

As we got dressed for KK's annual gala dinner at the Lake Club I yearned to wear my favorite dark green or deep magenta sari Papa had bought me years ago, but KK said those colors hurt his eyes. He insisted I tie one of the pastel ones he had got for me whenever I accompanied him. The border of my sari hem should sit just above the floor, neither sweeping it, nor too high above my sandals. When his rules were not met, KK made me untie my sari and redo it all over again. I wanted to scream at having to re-wrap and re-tie myself with six yards of cloth, but just smiled, as if to say I was sorry. Once, when I took too much time getting dressed, he drove off on his own, leaving me gasping and gaping. He didn't care about my feelings. What I minded most was that Thangachi, who should respect me as her elder sister, saw my humiliation during one of her many visits.

"Acca, small matter only. You have married such a handsome man who looks like my favorite Hollywood star Tyrone Power. He is also wealthy. So what if he has a few faults?" Although she was younger than me, sometimes I thought she seemed more worldly and wise - perhaps a bit too much.

That night I didn't want to be left behind, as not only were Thangachi and I to be seated with KK, but his lady friends from his club would also attend. Those European and Eurasian ladies, with sleeveless and strapless blouses, and God knows whatever-else-less, and Chinese ladies in tight cheongsams, with high slits at the sides, were all to be seated at the same dining table.

I noticed one scantily dressed young woman, in a bare-back, black see-through top with a short white lacy skirt, pushing her way through to be seated on KK's right. He even stood up to pull the chair out for her. When it was time for the group photograph she stood really close to KK as the photographer gestured us all to stand together. As Thangachi and I headed for the ladies powder room I deliberately let the long sequinned mundhani of my sari sweep over the woman's face, hoping it might scrape off some of her makeup. Thangachi saw this, and said she wasn't sure if I was more unhappy with KK or that woman. I slammed the toilet door. She put her hand on my shoulder and said, "Acca, I can see you are angry. Don't you think you are blessed that our KK asked me to marry him, rather than one of those boldly dressed women at our table?"

Although still upset, I had to admit that Thangachi was right. KK could have stepped out of our custom and married someone from outside the family, or even further away, one of those ladies from another race and religion. That new wife would have pushed me aside totally, as we would have been strangers to each other. I would have had no influence at all on her, whereas Thangachi, who calls me Acca, would show me much more respect as KK's first wife and her elder sister, the way no alien could do.

Barely a month later, after having been a bride myself seven years before, I saw myself in the mirror, leaning toward Thangachi to help her tie the pastel-blue wedding sari with golden embroidery our late Amma had given me as my heirloom when I came of age.

I arranged the mundhani so that the more intricate design from Amma's sari hung neatly over her shoulder. I consoled myself that if it wasn't Thangachi but some other bride I wouldn't even be allowed near the dressing room, and the new bride wouldn't be wearing anything like a sari. Yet I asked her, "Are you very sure you want to marry my husband?" The mirror reminded me of how the glow in me when I first got married had gone away. My loss of face in the past month showed physically. My face in the mirror was hollow and weary; it said to me that I was at a funeral, not a wedding.

As I tried to place an equal number of matching blue and gold bangles on Thangachi's wrists she squeezed my hands with her henna-stained fingers and said, "Acca don't worry, I will always obey you both."

I heard KK reciting the same vows of fidelity, love, and mutual respect, which he had made when he led me round the agni, sacred fire of ghee and wooden sticks, seven times, seven years before. But this time KK's little finger was clasping Thangachi's, and not mine. At the climax of the wedding ceremony, when KK tied the tali around Thangachi's neck, the accompanying mridangam, thavil drums, the Nadaswaran trumpets and temple bells rose simultaneously to a crescendo. As I continued standing behind Thangachi I felt I was choking with shame. I told myself that I had kept my vows intact, but this man hadn't and Thangachi was complicit.

To prove to me, to Thangachi, and to our community, that he was right in marrying her while I was still alive he was doing the kicking. KK had fasted, spread thicker strokes of vibuthi ash on his forehead, and made special poojas to Lord Ganesha to remove the obstacles to him being a father. He raised his long arms to the temple ceiling, then prostrated himself with his hairy bare chest on the floor as he pleaded loudly with Lord Ganesha for just one boon. His gestures were so over-eager they made him look clownish. He offered the kolukatai I had made for his pooja. I had offered special poojas too, with the softest, most evenly shaped, extra kolukatai, as they are Lord Ganesha's favorites. Unlike KK, I did it secretly. I didn't want to lose all of what was left of my face if my prayers were ignored.

Within a month, something happened that none of the three of us had ever dreamt of. First, I threw up. KK had dismissed it as something I must have eaten. As I settled on the sofa Thangachi teased me, "Acca I come into your family officially and so soon you are going to be a mother. I brought you luck."

Thangachi always took credit for all the good news in our family, so this remark was nothing new to me, but I was too happy to tell her that I had prayed to be a mother and at last I was to be an Amma, the most precious word I know. I smiled at each of Thangachi's continued self-praises.

Then, two weeks later, when Thangachi vomited, KK congratulated her. "This is most welcome morning sickness," he said. I wished I had thrown up on him. Our special poojas to Lord Ganesha had been answered more than once. He prayed to be a father and got to be one, two times over.

Many a time, KK rushed home from work, bringing with him piping hot vadai, served with red and green mint coconut chutney, and sweet purple yam porridge, and showed how excited he was to have bought all that Thangachi craved for. KK brought some over to my room, and I had to pretend not to notice they were cold leftovers from Thangachi's tea-time treat.

To compensate, I spoiled myself by having long hot baths in the mornings, gently scrubbing and massaging myself with a paste of bath powder mixture of sweet-scented sandalwood and saffron powder. Seated in front of my dressing table mirror, I dipped my thumb into my oval silver kumkum holder a few times, and took extra kumkum red powder for my forehead to be placed in front of my parting hairline.

When my contractions began, KK arranged for the driver to send me to the General Hospital to have my baby. I was in an empty double-room. As I looked through the window next to my bed I saw tall trees swaying in the wind, bringing my thoughts to names for my baby. They should start with the letter 'K' for KK. If it is a girl she should be named Kumari, and if a boy, then Kumar to match the father's name. I went into labor. I woke up a few hours later to see next to me a cot with my baby, Kumari, asleep and all wrapped up. She had my thick wavy hair. At each ring of the bell, the nurse came into my room asking me what I needed, before I was served hot Ovaltine and goreng pisang. It was nice there with Kumari and all these people who fussed over me; people I could speak to, who listened, and brought me whatever I needed.

Four days later, KK rushed in to tell me that Thangachi had complained of pains and might be in early labor. He brought her to the same hospital in his new car. Although the doctor told him it was a false alarm they decided to keep her in anyway, so she stayed there.

I just listened to what he said and saw how he rushed off to see her. He spent more time by her bedside than mine. The nurses thought he was Thangachi's husband and merely my relative.

Barely a week after my baby Kumari, hers was born. Thangachi sulked at my having my baby first. Then there was a big change. Thangachi was one up on me, as not only had she delivered a child for our husband, but one with a most vital gift.

One of the nurses wheeled me into Thangachi's room and I saw how KK had embraced her with such enthusiasm and lifted her baby, Raja, so high, because he was a boy. Thangachi was the mother of a champ, so that made her a champ too. When he had picked up my baby earlier he hadn't lifted her up anywhere as high, and he embraced me with less warmth. I felt it was a struggle not even to be seen as a runner-up with my contribution of a baby daughter. I also noticed that KK's late mother's heart-shaped emerald pendant and thick gold chain adorned Thangachi's now fat neck. I didn't sulk openly.

I was sent home with my baby first, and had two quiet days with Kumari, after which Thangachi returned from hospital, making her usual demands to KK in her shrill voice: "Please can you order sakarai satham, with extra brown sugar in the rice, crushed cardamom seeds, and roasted cashew nuts over it, and make sure you offer that as thanksgiving to Lord Ganesha for making you a father to our new-born son. After the blessing bring a small portion back for both of us please."

Unlike the past seven years, I saw a gentle smile on KK's face, and his temper had disappeared too. I saw him sitting on his usual sofa cooing to baby Raja.

Sometimes mothers die at childbirth, but this time it was the father who died of a heart attack within four weeks of our two babies being born. I'm glad that's one 'custom' that has changed in this man's world.

My friend Mrs. Chong said 'sei' in Cantonese meant both four and death. KK's doctor, who rushed over when he collapsed at home, said that despite his advice on how a heart patient should behave, KK had raised his voice to him, especially when he referred to KK as someone with a heart condition.

Now, at the funeral, as the hearse pulls up at our main gate, Thangachi beats her head with both her palms. "Kadavellai, my God, why did you do this to him just when you gave us our greatest miracle? You have given me a son, but you have taken away my husband."

I'm standing beside her, but she says "my", not "our" or "your" husband. I cannot wait to set her right after this melodrama is over. When we were little girls we played pura-pura, pretend-pretend games. She doesn't realize that she cannot continue to pretend that I don't exist in her life. All these months it has been herself, her son and KK, without any mention of her Acca. She seems so immersed in her grief that she barely notices my presence. She is wailing much louder than me for this man who gave me all the blame and took all the credit for himself and Thangachi. She has shown our relatives, KK's colleagues and friends, that he meant much more to her than to me. Why the need to parade ugly half-truths when I am the one who has cared for him all these years?

Our guests are slowly leaving. The white and yellow frangipani from the wreaths surrounding the main foyer are beginning to fade. Outside, the sky is turning blue with white clouds, and the sun is beginning to shine. I now have my daughter Kumari to care for, and soon a son too.

"The king is dead. Long live the queen." Since I heard that on BBC radio five years ago in 1952, when King George VI died and Princess Elizabeth took over as Queen, I've dreamt of this moment. This is my Merdeka.

"Now at last, I am the head of this household," I say when all the relatives, friends and neighbors have left. I go to our sitting room and am seated spread out on the sofa like KK used to be. Thangachi follows me and sits on the rug. Her cold fingertips touch my warm feet and bring my thoughts back to her. As she reaches up to hug me I push her forehead back. Shall I put Thangachi through all KK did to me?

"Too late for the old Acca business. Acca is dead, long live Amma. Now you have to pay me back."

"How Amma? I have nothing to give."

"Nothing? Is your son nothing?"

"Aiyo, no Amma. He's the only thing that I have."

"You took all that I had. You snatched my husband into your cradle. I saw after our son was born that you are no different from the women of other races in the club."

"I'm so sorry Amma. Aiyo, Amma."

Tears rolled down Thangachi's black eyeliner-smeared cheeks once again.

"Many poor mothers have given away their babies so their children may have a better life."

"They give away daughters for adoption but… but… never their sons, Amma."

"It's time to throw away the bad old man-made customs and start some new woman-made ones. You will announce to the world that I delivered twins, a girl and a boy."

"Now I'm beginning to understand this nightmare."

"Nightmare? You dare call my dream your nightmare?"

"Sorry Amma, I meant this change. Can I think about all you said, Amma?" Thangachi asked.

"Then I will think about whether I should kick you out of my house. By the way, I want to show you something at the top of the stairs."

"Aiyo, Amma you won't kick me down the stairs, the way Athan kicked the dhobi?" Thangachi lifts her other hand.

"What happened to the dhobi is nothing compared to what I will do to you," I say, as I lead her upstairs by her wrist.

PANOPTICON

VICTOR FERNANDO R. OCAMPO

"The illusion of free will is itself an illusion."
– Sam Harris, Neuroscientist and Author.

I woke up in a dirty public toilet, white noise fogging my head. The stink of urine and cigarettes choked the dead air. A broken sink in front of me lay thick with organic crust, ashes and ancient spittle. Overhead, an incandescent bulb flickered uncertainly.

"Mr. Salazar?" a voice behind me asked. "Try not to move so much, you're not complete yet."

I glanced up at the mirror and saw the reflection of a woman in a tight white jumper, slender and tall like a huntress. I knew immediately that something was wrong. Her face was familiar, too familiar. It was a face that I had seen hundreds of times before, the Singaporean screen siren Marrie Lee. She looked as if she'd stepped out from the movie *They Call Her Cleopatra Wong*.

I balled my hand into a fist. I knew she couldn't possibly be real.

"No need to fight Mr. Salazar. Your reaction is all the confirmation I need," the strange woman said. "Cigarette?"

"Who are you?" I asked, gagging at the assault of cesspool smells. "Where am I?"

"It's me, Pai Kia," the woman said, her voice dropping suddenly to a baritone. "I'm Ms. Esperanza's agent, remember? Let me adjust my HI."

"H… HI?" I stammered, as her body morphed into something more androgynous.

"Aiyoh. H-I, Haptic Interface, It allows you to touch me," e explained. "Anyway, we spoke at Golden Acres. I'm your caseworker, at least for the next few minutes. Sorry for the rough landing, this is my cheapest loading program. You did travel by steerage after all. Welcome to Alt.Tundon."

I threw up.

"Isn't it wonderful? That's your system getting rid of unnecessary information," Pai Kia said, as e took a drag from a long Djarum Black. "Feels so real, correct or not? This place is almost the real universe. You won't see any pixelation, not even at the quantum level. This hack is *that* good. You *gone case* uncle. But soon, very soon, you won't even remember transitioning."

I threw up until my knees gave way. My face slumped into the dirty sink, straight into the puddle of my own vomit.

"Listen, I'm paid by the second, so listen and listen closely," the agent said. "You just came back from the dead and your algorithm's still broken. She wants you to find her. This time she says there's less bullshit, no guns and no restraining orders. Find her. She's waiting for you."

"Where am I? What… what is this place?" I asked.

"Alt.Tundon's a Hacker Town. It's a cloud of parasite spaces called Gimokud, hidden beneath the New Cities. Are you sure you don't remember? The New Cities are what passes for Paradise for the affluent deceased."

Pai Kia fished for something in eir pocket and tossed it to the floor. It was an old Casio Databank watch.

"Since you're not part of the 1%, you have to wear one of these. Your identity and your credits are inside until you're re-skinned. Don't lose it or you'll be purged. If you need more credits you'll have to sell something. If you got nothing, sell yourself. Good luck."

"Wait..." I whispered hoarsely, struggling to my feet. "Please wait."

By the time I finally managed to stand, the agent was gone. Only the smell of clove cigarettes remained, pungent as rotting fruit.

I moved to a clean sink and washed my face. When I looked into the mirror, an impossible face stared back. I was young again, probably 41 or 42. That was about the age I was when I first met Esperanza. I had a feeling something would happen to my appearance when I transitioned, but I had not expected this.

Damn it. Why is she torturing me? Why now, after all these years? I felt a familiar flood of pain and self-loathing. *Why did I even come?*

In my old age I had tried my best to forget about her, to erase what had ripped my heart out. Our love broke me to the point where I couldn't deal with relationships, not anymore, perhaps not ever.

It took a long time, but after years I believed my nightmare was behind me. Why the hell did I agree to see her again? Why the hell did I agree to tear open old wounds?

It hadn't been easy. My stupid heart refused to forget past sins. To move on, I had opted to misremember everything. Memory was never perfect anyway, and false memories were just as good as real ones, if you wished hard enough.

I dried my face on my shirt. It was made of piña cloth, a luxurious Barong Tagalog reserved for weddings. The telltale static of Nanotex fabric on wet skin, a glitch actually, told me the shirt wasn't real. I put on the watch she'd left me and checked its digital signature. Every single thing I was wearing was a hand-me-down download, pre-owned by her dead husband, the industrialist Julio Salas.

A message scrolled across the calado embroidery on my shirt cuffs, a helpful reminder of my indigent humiliation:

> Good evening Mr. ~~Salas~~ Mr. Salazar.This shirt is best washed with Mr. Clean digital detergent. Removes vomit and all simulated organics.

A detergent ad? Biofilms and ultrasonics cleaned everything now and I hadn't seen real soap in decades. I decided it was probably a skeuomorph, a virtual anachronism designed to make people – old people – more comfortable being digitized.

What the hell is this place?

I staggered out of the toilet. Night had fallen and I looked around the deserted alley, wondering where I was supposed to go. A bicycle had been propped on a wall just in front of the lavatory entrance. As soon as I stepped toward it the bike began to flash its lights, illuminating layers of advertising graffiti with a frail white fluorescence. The lights kept blinking until I put my hand on its bamboo handlebars.

A message popped on its digital odometer:

Thank you for choosing a Shimano Intelligent Bicycle Mr. ~~Satas~~ Mr. Salazar. The seat has been automatically adjusted to your height. Your route has already been pre-selected. Please climb aboard and simply pedal.

I heaved myself onto the gel-padded saddle and kicked off. The bike guided me through the dark and narrow alleys that snaked through the labyrinth of tenements. Everything in Alt.Tundon lay in the shadow of its sole skyscraper, the neon-lit Torre Paraiso.

I passed through the slums like a ghost. Through the yawning windows I saw people leading seemingly normal lives – playing mahjong, or the card game pusoy dos, eating dinner, or simply gathered around their living rooms, plugged into a legion of electronic devices. This was a town of old people, permanently idle; permanently trapped in the amber of unstructured time. Not a single child was in sight.

The faces of certain strangers looked disturbingly familiar. I passed a panciteria, where I thought I saw Harrison Ford drinking San Miguel beer with Jonathan Pryce and Bembol Roco. Nearby, on a street-level TODA station, a woman the spitting image of the actress Hilda Colonel waited patiently for a hover-cyclo to come.

I wondered how many of them were *real* people, not background SIMs, or in-memoriam programs. If they were human, I wondered if this was their idea of heaven.

The bicycle took me away from the maze of small streets to a wide, tree-lined boulevard bustling with shops and post-modern apartments. My ride stopped in front of a garishly-lit clothing store called The Way We Wear. There, an oddly-dressed man waited expectantly.

"Welcome to Alt.Tundon, Mr. Salazar," he said softly. The old man wore a circus ringmaster's outfit. On his head was an elegant top hat with large aviator goggles hanging carelessly from its brim. A strange watch, encrusted with many dials, covered his left arm like an armature of metal eczema. I imagined it could keep time for the entire universe.

"I have been asked to dress you and guide you to Paraiso."

"Thank you, but this looks like an expensive place," I replied, as I stepped in to view his merchandise. The store smelled of spikenard, incense and myrrh, the stink of gods and rich people. "I'm not sure I have enough credits."

"Don't worry about that, Mr. Salazar," he reassured me. "Your re-skinning has already been paid for."

Inside the store I realized there were no actual clothes, just an infinite library of paintings, photos, and video screens, displaying clothing styles from every time period and from all over the world.

"Now then," he announced theatrically, "a Gimokud is a world where heart and mind are one."

"Hang on. What is this place?" I interrupted. "Where am I? Am I dead?"

"I understand that you were a filmmaker once," he said cryptically. "You were a director, a scriptwriter. You were once a *Creator*."

"Yes, but what does that have to do with anything?"

"Can you not recognize art when you see it? Some creators can build worlds from words and images. Some can create an entire universe. Your mind is what the philosopher Anaxagoras called '*the intellect that builds reality*'."

"You're not making any sense," I said. "Who built this? Who is responsible for this place?"

"I was under the impression that *you* were responsible," he announced without emotion. "I suppose if you want to know more, you will have to ask Mrs. Salas."

"Where is she?" I asked. "Is Esperanza really here?"

"She is waiting for you at Paraiso. I am afraid you are running very late."

I wasn't sure if it was my traumatic transition, or simply the thought of seeing Esperanza again, but I felt suddenly faint. I sat down on a huge Persian carpet in the center of the store and buried my head in my hands.

"I'm sorry. Please get up," the old man said gently. "Paraiso checks for broken souls and will frown on your second-hand clothes."

"I have nothing else."

"Oh, that is not true. Even here you have some measure of agency." he said unexpectedly. "I will use your Nanotex canvas to craft a new outfit that will map the man you used to be. I will cut it from the cloth of your pain, that buried fabric spun from the love you've lost and sew it with the dark threads of your forbidden consummations. Finally, I shall embellish it with the future fruit of your final, bittersweet meeting."

"What are you talking about?"

The older man was much stronger than he looked. He helped me up and ushered me to his workstation.

"Does that outfit sound about right to you?" he asked. "After all, our clothes are guideposts to our feelings. Your outside will now match what is inside. How are you feeling now Mr. Salazar?"

"I don't know," I answered. A swarm of 3D printers, buzzing like paper wasps, stripped me down to my bare Nanotex frame. There was absolutely nothing underneath.

"You are dressing me with emotions that I have spent a lifetime forgetting."

"Ah, but that is who you are," said the old man.

The tailor's curious machines repaired my algorithm, then created code by code, thread by thread, a beautiful new suit of gray merino wool – one that did not have *'Mr. Julio Salas'* crossed out on its digital signature.

"Perfect," the old man exclaimed. "As they say, clothes do make a man. You are now a perfect simulation of your old self. Perhaps this time you will find the right words to say."

"What do you mean?" I asked. "What do I need to do now?"

"Just a piece of advice – the body can become young again, but the soul, never. When the hurt is strongest we must watch what we say," he cautioned. "Now go please, there is a Personal Air Lifter outside, waiting to take you to Paraiso. Mrs. Salas is already there."

I thanked the old man and left feeling as gray as my suit. I wasn't really sure what he'd done, but it felt like I'd been prepped for a funeral.

"Hello again, Mr. Salazar," Pai Kia greeted cheerily, as I climbed aboard the sleek red aircraft. E was still dressed in Cleopatra Wong's tight white jump suit. "You clean up very nicely, Uncle. I could fancy someone like you."

I said nothing as our autogiro lifted toward an indifferent brown sky, past the grid of wires that stretched over the slums like a garrote. The highway in the heavens was teeming with sky jeeps, floating hawker stalls, hover-cyclos, air tuk-tuks, and giant advertising dirigibles. The latter's Holosonic displays bombarded my head with hundreds and thousands of advertisements, factoids, and subliminal purchasing suggestions.

I closed my eyes to escape, letting the lights of the airborne traffic blur into hazy constellations. Every few seconds, a small group of vehicles would peel away, puncturing the smoke-choked clouds like dying meteors.

"I don't get it," I asked. "If people pay to be here, why does it look like a retro-future dump? It's like we went back in time, to some old Third World country."

"Wah liao, every time the same questions," Pai Kia said. "Let me tell you all you need to know. Aiyoh, everyone has three possible after-lives. If you're rich, you stay in the clean, ultra-luxe New Cities. If you're poor, you just die, end of story. For everyone in between, if you're in the know and you've got something in the way of credits, you can pay soul-hackers like me to build an afterlife. But hey, as they say – *no prawns, fish also can*. Do you understand lah?"

I nodded for some reason, even though eir answer made no sense.

"Of course, your level of comfort, your level of reality, depends on the size of your wallet. Ms. Esperanza has a very big wallet."

I studied my strange companion, wondering how e really translated behind the HI. Was e even real? I couldn't tell anymore.

"Listen," Pai Kia said, with a voice that slid viscously, like snails gliding on glass. "I don't know why, but she instructed us not to complete you. I'm sure you already know. There's no kuku bird down there."

E pointed to my crotch, a sad, flat affair devoid of any protrusions.

"I can fix that. We can work something out."

I was way too tired to hide my emotions. I looked straight into eir eyes, sharing a yearning and a heartache that words simply could not convey.

"So drama, ah! Lucky woman, that Ms. Esperanza," Pai Kia laughed. "Aiyoh, the mosquito dies but the itch remains doesn't it? Nevertheless, my offer is there if you change your mind. My contact's in your watch."

We flew toward our destination in silence.

X

Torre Paraiso was a private Integrated Resort that rose seven kilometers into the heavens, the enormous building tessellated into separate sections that celebrated Christianity's Seven Deadly Sins: *Envy, Avarice, Gluttony, Sloth, Lust, Wrath* and *Pride*. Pai Kia dropped me off at the rooftop landing pad and blew me a kiss for luck.

Esperanza was waiting for me at the Immersion Gallery, an 8-Star lounge at the penthouse level. Everything inside was done in the old Filipino style called Earthquake Baroque. The rooms were hewn from pig-fat marble and solid piedra china, gaudy and over-the-top with decorative calabasa motifs. The transoms, fixtures and room detailing were all gilded with mother-of-pearl and electrum ormolu.

On the walls were Holosonic reproductions of early masterpieces – Lunas, Hidalgos, and Amorsolos, each one radiated terabytes of synesthetic information and shared emotional content. A large Luna, The Spoilarum, filled my mind with images of dying gladiators and left the unwelcome taste of blood in my mouth.

This was an area reserved exclusively for the most important of VIPs, the world's 1% mega-rich, members of an exclusive club called Pride.

Esperanza sat almost preternaturally still, like a porcelain doll, her small frame entombed within the red womb of a rare Cobonpue Ball Chair, woven from the finest, palest bamboo.

"Hello Alfredo," she whispered softly.

I said nothing and looked around the room until I found another Ball Chair to curl into. I hid my head in the cold shadows, not wanting her to divine my feelings. Esperanza looked exactly like she did when I first fell in love with her. Her short brown hair was cut in a bob, framing a delicate face that looked not unlike the 1970s actress Marrie Lee.

We sat across the room staring at each other for what seemed like hours. As each second passed, I pressed myself deeper into the chair's embrace. The weight of her presence slowly turned every bone in my body to glass.

"What is this place? Why did you bring me here?" I said finally, yielding to the oppressive stillness. "I was happy at Golden Acres. You should have let me die in peace."

"You'd rather be in a hospice ship?" she asked. "Death has no angels, you know. It has no dominion. There are no tunnels of light. There's just this or oblivion."

"This is nothing but another prison."

"Yet you still came when I called. Why?"

"I don't know."

"Do you still have feelings for me?" Esperanza asked. Behind the grottoes of her eyes I sensed the vague shine of emotions I thought she'd long forgotten (or maybe it was just a trick of the light?).

I took a deep breath and decided to say nothing. When I was alive, our past had kept me in a cell without walls. Words bled, words betrayed. I let the silence tell her everything she needed to know.

"Really, you have nothing to say to me?" Esperanza pressed; "after all this time?"

"Why am I here?" I whispered finally.

"Let's recap, shall we? I married Julio the year after you and I parted. He was so much older than you. He had money and best of all he never, ever hurt me. After that, I had ... I have a beautiful child. In fact my baby is having his own baby soon. For the last thirty years I've lived a blessed life, a life most people can only dream of."

"Why am I here Esperanza? Why can't anyone give me a straight answer?"

"Shut up and listen," she said. "That's always been your problem. You like simple answers because you don't like to listen."

I bit my lip and stared at her.

"Anyway, after Julio died, he transitioned to the New Cities and left me with so much. I hadn't planned to join him so soon, but there are things that no amount of money can control."

"I know all of this. I tried to come back to you but you took out a restraining order," I said cautiously, nervously. My skin wrinkled around me like a chrysalis. "I should have known enough to stay away."

"We left a lot of things unfinished, didn't we?" she added. I tried to search her eyes for a hint of what she was up to, but she quickly turned away. "Anyway, that money's what brought you here. I paid to capture a star that's keeping you alive. This storage facility's a town for hacked souls, true, and you're just a squatter under our New Cities. But you won't die, not for a very long time, and you'll never age. I can watch you whenever I want to, just like you used to watch me."

"Hang on, you *bought* me a star?"

"Yes, isn't that the kind of over-the-top melodrama you used to like?" she said. "Do you know how much processing power your brain needs? It takes the power of an entire star to store a single mind. That's why only the rich live can live forever."

"Why did you do this? This is really messed up, even for you. Did you even think to ask how I would feel?"

"I was seventeen, you were 42. That wasn't messed up? Did you ever consider me, or how *I* would feel?" she snapped. Her eyes rolled up to the ceiling, as if looking for something solid to hang onto. "You were my film teacher so I had this place built just for you. Doesn't it look like a set from your favorite movies? What were they again? I only remembered *Brazil*, *Blade Runner*, and *Manila in the Claws of Light*. You've always wanted to play the tragic hero. Well, my money can buy a lot of things."

"Why are you doing this? Why am I here?" I asked again. "It's not as if we have anything anymore. We made a mistake ... I made a mistake but, Jesus; that was a lifetime ago."

"And Jesus said we must pay for our mistakes."

"The truth is," I said crossly, "you were never the type to love anyone. You just liked to own people."

"Hah! Now who'd like to own a loser like you?" Esperanza yelled, losing her carefully-constructed cool. She closed her eyes and began to laugh.

"Stop it. Stop laughing please."

"As it happens, I *do* love someone, and the one that I love is my son," she declared, getting up from her chair. She snapped her long, slim fingers, and a viewing screen appeared on one of the filmy silver walls. "I promised him he would meet you one day but I had an unscheduled aneurysm. I guess this was the next best arrangement. At least now he can see you exactly as I once did."

A dark figure flickered on the screen, throbbing like a haunted memory.

"What happened to you Teacher Alfredo? You threw your life away, a burned-out basket case in a nursing home. It was lucky my agent found you before you died," she said, shaking her head in the manner of parents scolding their children.

Esperanza's tone became unexpectedly softer. "I took out that restraining order to save your life you stupid idiot. That's one more you owe me. Julio's extremely jealous. He would've killed you if he knew what you'd left me."

"What are you talking about?"

"Jun – *Julio Sales Jr.*" Esperanza addressed the dark figure looming through the static. "Speak now. You can translate into this Haptic Interface when I'm done."

The screen blinked like the eye of a god, exact and infallible, revealing painful truths. I had never seen her child. Esperanza paid big money to keep her family out of the press. But as soon as I saw his face, my knees buckled. Jun looked almost exactly like I did in my thirties.

"As you already know, this old man is your real father," she said haltingly. For a moment her voice seemed to betray the pain of a great, long-hidden loss. I waited for some real change, for forgiveness but Esperanza just pressed on coldly. "I would have rather you never met. But I made you a promise and your mama always keeps her promises. Take a good long look sweetie."

I tried to open my mouth but no words would come. My sentences seemed to stall in mid-thought.

The past belonged to the past, yet here we were now. Through the cybernetic agency of the Gimokud, a network of Dyson bubbles – huge, star-eating comput-ers storing souls in their pure mathematical form – we were young again; keeping secrets, and being every bit as hurtful as old times. It was a new kind of hell for the downloaded dead.

"Poor Julio never knew he was impotent," she said caustically. "You told me once that '*the seeds of obsession grow quickly to hate*' and that's all you need to know."

"Did … did you ever really love me Esperanza?" I stammered, fearing any answer she would give. The invisible bars of my newest cage began to reveal themselves in earnest. "You know, before things fell apart, you promised me forever."

"Even I can't afford more than one Eternity. Consider your star my repayment for your parting '*gift*'. You're alive as long as it's alive. And, oh yes, you wanted to be alone? Everyone here's a skeuomorph and this world is as empty as a Holosonic. You've got nine *billion* years to figure it all out."

Esperanza's form wavered strangely, fading in and out like a ghost. She disappeared, leaving no answers. On the silver screen, a man with a sad face full of burning questions, waited patiently for me to talk.

But before I could say anything, Esperanza reappeared and clipped a teleport cheat-band to my wrist.

"One day you actually need to keep your promise, Mother," the man on the screen said, making a sigh of tired resignation. "How many times do you need to do this before it's enough? I'm not getting any younger."

"I'm sorry son," Esperanza muttered as she and I disappeared, transmuted into floating-point equations inside the Gimokud's enormous brain. "Hell hath no fury *yada yada yada* … I still can't help the way I feel."

Next thing I knew we were back on Paraiso's rooftop landing pad.

"I forgot to give you this," Esperanza said, smashing my chin with a strong right cross.

I toppled from the edge of the platform, down into the darkness. I fell for a very long time, my body folding, breaking, and decaying into an endless rain of remorse and bitter ash that lasted nine billion years.

When I came to, I found myself in a dirty public toilet, white noise fogging my head. The stink of urine and cigarettes choked the dead air. A broken sink in front of me lay thick with organic crust, ashes and ancient spittle. Overhead, an incandescent bulb flickered uncertainly.

BIOS

Dean Francis Alfar is a Filipino playwright, novelist and writer of speculative fiction. His work has appeared in *Strange Horizons, Rabid Transit* and the *Exotic Gothic* series. He wrote the novel *Salamanca* (Ateneo Press, 2006), and three collections of short fiction. He edits the *Philippine Speculative Fiction* series, and is also a comic book creator.

Marc de Faoite was born in Dublin and lives in Malaysia. His short stories and essays have been published in Malaysia, Singapore, India, France, and Ireland. *Tropical Madness*, a collection of his short stories published by Fixi Novo, was longlisted for the 2014 Frank O'Connor International Short Story Prize.

Zedeck Siew used to work in the Malaysian media, for publications like *Kakiseni, The Nut Graph*, and *Poskod.my*. As part of the CENTAUR games collective he co-designed POLITIKO, a card game about Malaysian party politics. He is currently working on his first book, an illustrated catalog of imaginary Southeast Asian animals.

Raymond G. Falgui teaches English Literature at the University of the Philippines. His fiction has appeared in magazines such as *Philippines Free Press, Philippines Graphic*, and *Playboy Philippines*; his interest in mythology is reflected in short stories that have been published in *Kuwento: Lost Things, The Mythic Circle, Innsmouth Free Press, Digest of Philippine Genre Stories, Philippine Speculative Fiction III* and *V*, and *Alternative Alamat* (the last three are available in e-book format on Amazon).

Lyana Shah is a full-time copywriter living in Singapore, although she was born in Malaysia and grew up in Brunei. In her free time, she writes novels, kills video game zombies and enjoys a good cup of tea. She believes that talking is good, but writing is better.

Dipika Mukherjee is a writer and sociolinguist. Her debut novel, *Thunder Demons* (Gyaana 2011), was long-listed for the Man Asian Literary Prize; it has been republished (Repeater, UK) and distributed by Penguin/Random House worldwide as *Ode to Broken Things*. She also won the 2014 Gayatri GaMarsh Memorial Award for Literary Excellence.

Timothy L. Marsh holds a doctorate in Creative Writing from the University of Wales Aberystwyth. His work has appeared in *Ninth Letter, Barrelhouse, Fourth River, The New Welsh Review* and *The Los Angeles Review*. He has been a Tennessee Williams Scholar at the Sewanee Writers' Conference and a Graduate Exchange Scholar at Auburn University. In 2015 he served as the Hub City Press Writer-in-Residence.

Richard Calayeg Cornelio is a nineteen-year-old doing a BS in Materials Engineering at the University of the Philippines, Diliman. He has finished a fifteen-page paper for a film class on his laptop inside a moving bus, binge-watched an entire season of *Lost* the night before a major exam, which he miraculously passed, but he still cannot, for the life of him, write a short story without sitting on it for weeks. Also, he's a chronic crammer.

When the missus tells him to, **Ted Mahsun** takes out the trash while trying not to let her hear him grumble about it. Otherwise he keeps busy writing fiction, of which some can be found in *Cyberpunk: Malaysia*, *Hungry in Ipoh*, and *Griffith Review 49: New Asia Now Vol 2*.

Eliza Vitri Handayani has published short stories, essays, and translations in respected Indonesian literary outlets, as well as in the *Asia Literary Review, Griffith Review*, and *Asymptote Journal.* Her novel *From Now On Everything Will Be Different* came out in 2015 by Vagabond Press.

Michael Aaron Gomez is a prose writer from the Philippines. His work has appeared in magazines and journals. He has also been a fellow to two national writers' workshops. He lives in Dauin, Negros Oriental.

Tilon Sagulu is a Malaysian Dusun writer from Sabah. He was born Herlveron Bin Sagulu, but goes by the nickname he grew up with, Tilon (derived from a Dusun word, Guntialon, which means mischievous). He is currently pursuing an M.A in English Literature at University of Malaya.

Alexander Marcos Osias frequently explores science fiction & fantasy worlds – his work has been published in print and online markets, and he's co-edited one of the *Philippine Speculative Fiction* volumes. After living in various countries, he now resides in the Philippines with his lovely wife and rambunctious son.

Nin Harris is a Malaysian poet, writer, and Gothic scholar. Nin writes Gothic fiction, cyberpunk, nerdcore post-apocalyptic fiction, planetary romances and various other forms of hyphenated weird fiction. Nin's publishing credits include: *Jabberwocky 3, Goblin Fruit, Strange Horizons, Lackington's, Giganotosaurus*, and *Alphabet of Embers.*

Francis Paolo Quina teaches at the Department of English and Comparative Literature at the University of the Philippines Diliman campus. He is currently taking up his Master's degree in Creative Writing from the same university.

M. SHANmughalingam's stories and poems were published/ broadcast by BFMradio, British Council, Dewan Bahasa, EPB, EvansBros, Fish, Harvard University, Heinemann, Maya, MPH, Oxford University, Pearson-Longman, Penguin, Radio Fremantle, Silverfish, WordWorks, ZI; in Australia, France, India, Ireland, Malaysia, Singapore, UK and US. Website: http://www.drshantri.com

Victor Fernando R. Ocampo is a Singapore-based Filipino writer. His writing has appeared in *Apex Magazine, Strange Horizons*, and *The Quarterly Literature Review of Singapore*, as well as anthologies like the *Best New Singapore Short Stories, Lontar: The Journal of Southeast Asian Speculative Fiction*, and the *Philippine Speculative Fiction* series.